삭매와 자미

아시아에서는 《바이링궐 에디션 한국 대표 소설》을 기획하여 한국의 우수한 문학을 주제별로 엄선해 국내외 독자들에게 소개합니다. 이 기획은 국내외 우수한 번역가들이 참여하여 원작의 품격을 최대한 살렸습니다. 문학을 통해 아시아의 정체성과 가치를 살피는 데 주력해 온 아시아는 한국인의 삶을 넓고 깊게 이해하는 데 이 기획이 기여하기를 기대합니다.

Asia Publishers presents some of the very best modern Korean literature to readers worldwide through its new Korean literature series 〈Bilingual Edition Modern Korean Literature〉. We are proud and happy to offer it in the most authoritative translation by renowned translators of Korean literature. We hope that this series helps to build solid bridges between citizens of the world and Koreans through a rich in-depth understanding of Korea.

바이링궐 에디션 한국 대표 소설 084
Bi-lingual Edition Modern Korean Literature 084

Sakmae and Jami

김별아

삭매와 자미

Kim Byeol-ah

ASIA
PUBLISHERS

Contents

삭매와 자미

Sakmae and Jami

후한(後漢) 헌제(獻帝) 때 감숙성 돈황 사람으로 자는 언의(彦義)요, 이름은 삭매인 장수가 있었다. 그는 우람하나 비대하지 않은 팔 척 장신의 거구로, 반듯하고 평편한 뺨에 고향 땅 명사산의 준령처럼 콧대가 우뚝했다. 또한 높은 이마의 그늘 아래 눈동자는 사막을 거룩하게 하는 월아천(月牙川)의 샘물처럼 정하게 빛났으니, 과연 융준용안(隆準龍顔)의 호남아라 할 만했다.

변방의 사내였던 그가 수도 낙양에 입성한 때는, 황천태평(黃天泰平)의 구호를 내세우고 전국을 황하의 진흙물처럼 누렇게 휩쓴 농민기의군이 7주 28군에서 동시

During the reign of Emperor Xian of the Later Han Dynasty, there was a general called Sakmae, with the adult name of Yanyi, from Dunhuang in Gansu Province. He was a brawny, though not obese, man who was eight feet tall, and he had fine, even cheeks and a high, shapely nose, like the steep range of Singing Sand Mountain at his hometown. Under the shadow of his high forehead were eyes that shone as brightly as the spring water of Crescent Lake. He indeed deserved to be called a high-nosed, dragon-eyed, handsome man.

It was a time of rebellion when he had entered the capital Luoyang from that peripheral area.

에 기의하였던 변란의 시기였다. 이때 삭매의 나이 열일곱이었다. 천제의 부름에 의해 삼변(三邊)의 수속지병(殊俗之兵)으로 원정하여 황건에 대응했던 삭매는, 난이 진압되자 그 용맹함과 뛰어난 지략을 인정받아 수도를 호위하는 관군으로 편입되었다.

그는 낙양에서 큰 환대를 한 몸에 받았다. 물론 전쟁터에서 세운 공과 덕택이기도 했으나, 그의 이름을 더욱 드높인 것은 그에 대한 여인들의 열렬한 관심이었다. 그가 저자에 나서면 어느 사이 소식이 퍼졌는지 여인들이 구름처럼 몰려들어 그의 용태와 면면을 살폈다. 그가 지나는 곳마다 남몰래 그에 대한 소문을 소곤거리는 제비 떼 같은 소녀들의 지저귐이 그치지 않았다. 사내들조차 연적(戀敵)에 대한 원망과 질투조차 잊은 듯 넋을 놓고 그의 아름다운 모습을 바라보았다. 그럼에도 삭매의 언동은 언제나 한결같았다. 그의 얼굴에는 표정이 거의 없었다. 그는 따라 좇는 사병들의 걸음보다 배는 넓은 성큼한 보폭으로 뚜벅뚜벅 걸으며 묵묵히 자신의 책무를 이행할 뿐이었다. 그 뜨겁고도 냉랭한 태도에 여인들은 먼발치에서 훔쳐만 볼 뿐, 어설픈 웃음으

Armies of peasant rebels, rallied around the creed "Peace under the Yellow Heavens," arose in seven provinces and twenty-eight counties at the same time and swept over the entire country, like the muddy waters of the Yellow River. At the time, Sakmae was seventeen. Summoned by the emperor, he had joined the expeditionary force of the ethnic peoples from the three border areas to fight against the yellow-hooded rebels. After the insurrection was quelled, he was recognized as a brave and resourceful warrior and assigned to the government troops in defense of the capital.

He was warmly received by the people in Luoyang. Of course it was because of his distinguished services in the battlefield; but what helped him more to make a name was the zealous attention from the womenfolk. Whenever he strolled into the marketplace, it took no time for many women to get wind of the news and throng to see his handsome face and fine figure. Wherever he went, there were endless, furtive whisperings among young women, like a flock of swallows, spreading rumors about him. Even men would forget about their jealousy and grudges against him, their arch love rival, and gaze at his beautiful figure in a trance.

로 눈이라도 맞춰볼 생각조차 하지 못했다.

언젠가 한번은 시장 어귀에서 삭매에게 사과를 던진 여인이 있었다. 척과만거(擲果滿車), 시골의 풍속으로 여자가 사모하는 남자에게 과일을 선물해 구애하는 일을 가리킴이었다. 진나라의 반악은 대단한 미소년으로, 외출해서 낙양의 큰길을 걸을 때면 심지어 늙은 할머니들까지도 과일을 던져 그의 수레가 과일로 가득 찼다 하였다. 하지만 그 또한 옛이야기일 뿐, 지금 낙양의 거리 한복판에서 남자에게 과일을 던지는 여자는 찾아볼 수 없었다.

짐짓 다른 볼일이 바쁜 듯, 삭매에게 끌려가는 시선을 가누지 못하던 여인네들의 입에서 절로 '어머!' '아!' 하는 신음이 흘러나왔다. 그리고 곧 투척의 장본인에게 시선이 빠르게 옮겨져, 얼마는 눈살을 찌푸리고, 또 다른 얼마는 어이없는 헛웃음을 터뜨렸다. 삭매에게 사과를 던진 여인은 다름 아닌 시장의 명물 광란녀(狂亂女)였다. 하지만 삭매는 당황하는 빛도 없이 자신의 넓은 등을 맞추고 떨어진 시든 사과를 주워들었다. 그리고 아주 짧은 순간 물끄러미 그 쭈글쭈글하고 못난 과일을 쳐다

Despite their attention, Sakmae's speech and behavior never changed. He wore almost no expression on his face. He would stride on at a pace twice as long as that of his men, following behind him, and quietly carry out his duties. His intense and yet indifferent attitude kept the women from approaching him; no one dared to attempt even a hint of smile at him.

But once a woman threw an apple at Sakmae at the entrance to the marketplace. It was called "Toss-Fruit-Fill-The-Cart," part of the rural customs that allowed a woman to give fruit to a man she loved as a courting gesture. In the era of the Jin Dynasty, there had lived a boy named Ban'ak. He was so handsome that whenever he walked along the broad way of Luoyang, many women, even old ones, would toss fruit into his cart, quickly filling it to the brim. However, that was an old tale; now, no woman was seen tossing fruit to a man in the middle of a street in Luoyang.

The other women, who though pretending to mind their own business, could not help stealing glimpses of Sakmae and uttering "Ah!" and "Oh!" under their breath, quickly turned their eyes on the apple-tosser. Some of them frowned, while others

보더니, 이윽고 한일자로 굳게 다문 입을 벌려 절반쯤을 뭉텅 베어 물었다. 광기에 일을 벌여놓고도 한바탕 치도곤이 떨어질세라 겁에 질려 떨고 있던 광란녀가 흐르륵 깔깔깔, 우는 듯 웃었다. 삭매는 아무 일도 없었다는 듯 다 베어 먹은 응어리를 던져버리고 뚜벅뚜벅 제 갈 길로 걸어 사라졌다. 그 후 한동안 저잣거리는 삭매의 침착함과 호방함에 대한 칭송으로부터 삭매의 두툼하고 묵직한 입술 속에 숨은 고른 치열의 백옥 같은 이에 대해서까지, 덧붙여져 과장된 이야기로 한바탕 떠들썩하였다.

삭매에 대한 소문은 담장을 넘고 수렴을 헤쳐 호강지주(豪强地主) 여씨의 딸 향(香)의 귀에까지 닿았다. 향에게는 이미 좌청(左請)이란 약혼자가 있었으니, 향이 그에게 물었다.

"당신이 남의 이목 한가운데서 광란녀에게 척화만거를 당한다면, 당신은 어찌하려오?"

좌청이 느닷없는 질문에 불쾌한 기색을 감추지 못하고 답했다.

"군자를 모욕하였으니 광란녀는 형을 받아야 하리. 대

laughed, dumbfounded. The apple-tosser was none other than a deranged woman known to everyone in the marketplace. Showing no sign of fluster, Sakmae picked up the apple that had fallen to the ground, after hitting his broad back. He looked at the withered, wrinkled apple for just a moment, then opened his mouth, which had been kept firmly closed, and took almost half the apple in one bite. The deranged woman, although she had thrown the apple out of sheer madness, was trembling in fear, as if she knew a severe punishment was awaiting her. When she saw Sakmae eating the apple, however, she let out what sounded like both a cackle and a sob. After he finished eating the apple, Sakmae threw away the core and strode away, as if nothing had happened. For a while after the incident, the marketplace was clamorous with praises of Sakmae's composure, openheartedness, even rows of white, jade-like teeth, hidden inside his thick and reticent lips, and other exaggerated talk.

Rumors about Sakmae spread along the grapevine, over the fences, and into the private chambers, finally reaching the ear of Xiang, the daughter of the most-powerful landowner Lu's. Xiang was

벽(大辟)의 극형에 유폐(幽閉)의 중형을 부과해야 마땅할 일이나, 당자가 광란녀임을 고려해 곤(髡)의 형으로 그를 다스리리다."

"장자는 당비당차(螳臂當車)라 하여 분수를 모르고 덤빔을 경계하였으나, 당대의 형국이 어찌 광란녀만을 당랑이라 하고 성벽에 둘러싸여 사병에게 호위받는 우리를 차바퀴라 장담하리오?"

향은 그 자리에서 좌청과의 혼약을 파기하고 삭매에게 혼담을 넣을 매파를 불렀다. 하지만 낙양의 생활에 염증을 느끼던 삭매는 곧 수도 수호의 영이 끝나고 본래의 임무에 복귀하리라는 것을 이유로 정중히 청혼을 거절하였다. 그 후로 삼 일이 채 지나지 않았을 때, 삭매는 다시 천제의 영을 받아 관할지의 수장으로 임명되었다. 더 이상 여씨녀의 청혼을 거절할 명분이 없어진 것이었다.

향은 이백여 경의 토지를 경작하는 대부호 여건(呂虔)의 소생으로, 본디 고명딸이었으나 사내아이의 명운이 짧은 집안의 내력으로 남자 형제들을 모두 잃고 홀로 남은 외딸이었다. 향은 삭매보다 한 살이 많은 열여덟

already engaged to a man named Zuo Qing. One day, she asked him:

"If the deranged woman threw an apple at you in front of all those people, what would you do?"

Zuo Qing, unable to hide his displeasure at the unexpected question, answered:

"The deranged woman must be punished for insulting a gentleman. Either having her beheaded or thrown in jail would be an appropriate punishment, but considering she is a deranged woman, I would just have her hair shaved."

"Although Chuang Tzu warns against indiscretion in his parable of a mantis attacking a wagon wheel with its forelegs, considering today's situation, we cannot safely liken the deranged woman to a mantis, and us, protected by the soldiers and the castle wall, to a wagon wheel, can we?"

On the spot, Xiang broke off her engagement to Zuo Qing and summoned a matchmaker who would carry her proposal of marriage to Sakmae. But Sakmae had felt tired already of the life in Luoyang and politely refused the marriage proposal, saying that he would go back to his previous post after his term of duty in the capital was over. Less than three days later, though, Sakmae was ap-

나이로, 일찍이 아비의 장원에서 말을 달리며 작물의 재배와 야철을 지휘하여 자산을 늘리는 데 일조한 여걸이었다. 그녀는 폐월수화(閉月羞花)의 빼어난 미인이었으나 성품이 냉정하고 머리가 비상했다.

대장원을 경영하는 데는 무장이 필수적이었다. 향토를 지배하고 불합리한 정령(政令)에 항거하기 위해서는 칼과 창이 재보의 무게를 받쳐주어야 했다. 여씨의 장원에도 환수대도(環首大刀)로 무장한 병장(兵長)이 있었으나, 아무리 그 기상이 사내의 뺨을 친다 하여도 아녀자의 몸으로 군을 지휘하기엔 한계가 있었다.

삭매는 훌륭한 지휘관이요, 동업자였다. 무인의 기질을 타고난 삭매는 병장의 지휘에 역할을 다하는 한편, 혼돈의 정치사 한가운데에서 여씨 일족이 무사히 가계와 재화를 보존하는 데 일조하였다. 하루아침에 나라의 주인이 바뀌고 어제의 동지가 오늘의 적이 되는 수상한 시절에도, 여씨의 대장원에는 울창한 수목 아래 방목된 가축들이 살찌고 비옥한 토지에서 생산된 곡물과 재화들이 성시(城市)를 장악하였다.

그러나 정작 최고의 행운아로 칭송받는 삭매의 심기

pointed by the emperor as the head of the military jurisdiction he belonged to. Now, he had no cause to refuse the marriage proposal from the Lu family, so Xiang and Sakmae were married.

Xiang's father, Lu Qian, was a very wealthy man, with some 200 *gyongs* of farming land. And Xiang was Lu's only child. Lu had had sons, but it ran in the family that sons died young, and all of them had died, leaving Xiang alone. She was eighteen, a year older than Sakmae, and had played a crucial role in building up the family fortunes by riding all over her father's land on horseback, directing the cultivation of crops and the iron-refining herself. She was an outstanding beauty, who put the moon and flowers to shame, but also composed and keen-witted.

Having a warlord was essential to running a large-scale manor like Lu's. In order to keep its native province under control, and to counter unreasonable government ordinances, the manors needed swords and spears to buttress the weight of their riches. The Lu family manor was also manned with soldiers armed with fine, ring-pommeled long swords. Nevertheless, even when Xiang's valiant spirit outshone the men's, there was

는 적이 편치 못하였다. 저택의 동(棟)이 수백으로 연이어져 있고 토지가 뜰에 가득하며 노비가 수천으로 헤아려지는 대장원 속에서도 답답한 마음은 가시지 않았다. 아내 향과 일곱 명의 자식들은 나고 자란 태생이 그러하여서인지, 갇힌 장원의 군주로 군림하며 사는 일에 아무런 불편도 없어 보였다. 하호(下戶)와 노비를 부리는 일에서도 마찬가지였다.

언젠가 삭매는 맏아들 웅(雄)이 말가죽 채찍으로 제 몸종을 사납게 후려치는 모습을 보았다. 웅의 몸종은 태어난 지 삼칠일도 지나지 않아 제 어미의 젖을 갓난 웅에게 빼앗긴 유모의 아들이었다. 복종의 미덕 하나로 평생을 버텨온 우직한 어미 덕택에 자른 탯줄이 말라 떨어지기도 전에 빈 젖의 허기를 운명처럼 감내해 온 천자(賤子)의 등판에 감겨든 채찍이 붉은 화인을 찍고 있었다.

"무엇 때문에 그러냐?"

신음 소리 하나 새어 내보내지 못하고 달팽이처럼 몸을 웅크려 앉은 몸종 아이의 모습을 지켜보기 딱하여 삭매가 나섰다. 웅은 아비의 부름에 잠시 채찍질을 멈

a limit to her ability as a woman to take command of the private army.

Sakmae became a great leader and a business partner for the family. Born with the warrior's temperament, he did his utmost as the commander of the family's troops, while playing an essential role in protecting the Lu family and preserving its riches in the midst of the political turmoils of uncertain times, when the ruler of a country changed overnight and yesterday's comrade turned into an enemy today. Despite the volatile socio-political circumstances, the cattle inside the Lu family manor were fattening, while freely grazing under the thick canopy of trees, and the crops and other riches of the family's fertile land dominated the streets of the walled city.

However, Sakmae, who was acclaimed as the luckiest man on earth, was in an ill humor. The premises of the great manor consisted of hundreds of buildings and large gardens and yards, taken care of by thousands of serfs. Yet Sakmae couldn't help feeling stifled in the manor. His wife and their seven children, born into wealth, seemed to have no problem living as rulers inside the manor, much the same way they worked their serfs and the low-

추고 벅차오른 숨을 씩씩거리며 대답하였다.

"도환(跳丸) 놀이를 하고 있는데, 이놈이 굴려 보낸 공을 찾아오라는 명을 제대로 받잡지 못하고—."

"도련님! 아무리 찾아도 공은 보이지 않습니다. 아마도 수련 못 늪지에 빠진 것이 분명합니다."

그제야 피투성이가 되어 있던 몸종 아이가 삭매와 웅을 동시에 바라보며 말했다. 동정을 호소하는 그 눈은 사시가 되어 불안하게 흔들리고 있어 더욱 바라보기 애처로웠다.

"이놈이 아직도 정신을 못 차리고, 공이 늪에 빠진 걸 안다면 건져 와야 옳지 않겠나? 감히 주인의 명을 거스르고도 네가 살기를 바라느냐?"

"늪의 깊이는 제 힘으로 차마 헤아릴 수 없으니, 도련님, 차라리 저를 벌해 주십시오!"

몸종 아이는 체념한 듯 다시 사지를 옹송그리고 몸을 굴려 매질에 익숙해진 자세를 취해 보였다.

"그만 하여라! 네게 남은 공은 얼마든지 있지 않느냐?"

삭매는 웅을 나무라기조차 포기한 채 한숨을 쉬며 말

er-class people.

Once, Sakmae saw his eldest son Xiong flogging his personal servant hard with a horse-hide whip. The servant was the son of Xiong's wet nurse, and had been deprived of his mother's milk when he was less than three weeks old; newly born Xiong, on the other hand, grew up suckling at his wet nurse's breast. Thanks to the simple-hearted wet nurse, who had borne all the hardships observing the virtues of obeisance, the servant boy had accepted the empty breast and hunger pangs as his fate from the days his umbilical cord hadn't dried yet. Upon that ill-fated, lowly boy's back the fiery whip came down, inscribing crimson brands on it.

"What is the matter?" Sakmae asked his son.

Unable to watch any longer, with the servant boy crouching on the floor like a snail, not even daring to groan, Sakmae stepped in. Hearing his father's question, Xiong stopped whipping and answered, panting hard:

"I was playing with a ball. I rolled the ball away, then asked this stupid donkey to go fetch it. But he failed to do my bidding."

"Please, Young Master! I have looked everywhere for it, but I could not find it. I believe it has fallen

했다. 웅은 아비를 이해할 수 없다는 듯이 의혹의 눈길로 쳐다보았다. 삭매는 포악과 오만으로 일그러진 아들의 얼굴을 짐짓 외면하였다. 은기(恩紀)라 하여, 다스림에 인정이 있을지라도 법은 굽히지 않음을 원칙으로 하였으나 실상은 인정 없이 가혹한 법만 횡행하였다. 마치 죄인을 몽둥이로 때려죽임이 참수보다 피를 덜 흘리기에 자비롭다며 장살(杖殺)의 처형 방식을 칭송한 관료들의 위선과도 같았다.

지독한 피로감뿐이었다. 충성을 다하여 따르기로 맹세한 주군들의 면면은 세월에 따라 시시각각 바뀌어갔고, 격랑 속에 몸을 보존하기가 아슬아슬한 줄 위를 걷는 듯하였다. 위로는 눈치를 보며 아첨하고, 아래로는 채찍을 들고 사람의 맨살을 쳤다. 어린 나이에 종군하여서는 미처 깨닫지 못했던 바, 결국 황건적의 난도 피폐한 삶을 견디지 못한 농민들이 살길을 찾듯 태평도(太平道)의 뜻에 의지함에 다름 아니었다.

소민(小民)의 폭동은 풀과 같아 밟아도 다시 살아나고
머리는 닭 같아서 잡아도 다시 운다.

into the water lily pond."

Only then did the blood-covered servant boy look at both Sakmae and Xiong. His eyes, desperate to win his masters' sympathy, narrowed and wavered anxiously, which made him look even more pathetic.

"You still don't know what you've done wrong, do you? If you knew that the ball was in the bog, you should have fetched it from the water. Do you wish to stay alive after you disobeyed your master's order like that?"

"I do not know how deep the bog is. So please, young master, I had rather you punished me!"

The servant boy seemed to have given up all hope, as he curled himself up on the floor in his all-too-accustomed posture, ready to receive the beating.

"Now, that is enough! You still have so many other balls." Sakmae said with a sigh, having given up even reproaching his son.

Unable to understand his father, Xiong looked confused and doubtful. Sakmae averted his eyes from his son's face, which was twisted with cruelty and arrogance. The governing principle at the time was "benevolent rule, but strict observance of

관리를 경외할 필요도 없고

민(民)을 가볍게 여길 필요도 없다.

수해와 한해, 황재(蝗災)와 지진의 공포 속에서 엄중한 부역과 질병과 기근에 시달리다 제 살던 땅을 버리고 떠도는 유민(流民)들의 가요가 귓가에 쟁쟁했다. 피의 보복으로 시신이 산을 이루던 그때의 참상을 생각하며 삭매는 다시금 치를 떨었다. 그날이 언제고 다시 오지 않으리라 확신할 수 없다. 그때라면 삭매는 다시 칼과 창을 잡고 양민들을 학살할 것이다. 평생을 살아온 방식대로, 주저 없이 싸우고 또 싸울 것이다. 그리고 반월도를 휘둘러 떨어뜨린 목만큼 창고에 쌓여가는 곡물과 보화를 볼 것이다.

삭매는 주군에 충성하고 명령에 복종하는 장수의 길을 걷기에 변함없이 충실하였으나, 마음속의 번민까지 멸진할 수는 없었다. 그럴수록 말수만 점점 줄어들 뿐이었다. 세월의 풍파에 연마된 연륜의 풍모에 고독경(孤獨境)에 이른 침묵이 덧붙여져, 삭매는 가히 범접하기조차 어려운 위엄을 얻게 되었다. 모두가 삭매를 두

laws." In reality, it was all severe laws and no mercy. This was evinced in the hypocrisy practiced by the bureaucrats who praised the punishment of clubbing to death as being more benevolent than beheading because the former shed less blood.

Sakmae felt only terrible fatigue. The attitude of the lords to whom he had pledged his loyalty changed from moment to moment; preserving one's life in the raging waves of the time was like walking on a tightrope. Quickly finding out how the wind blows, people curried favor with their superiors, while wielding whips on the bare skin of their inferiors.

While serving at the front as a young man, Sakmae had failed to realize the fact that the insurrection of the so-called yellow-hooded thieves had been merely a way of survival chosen by the peasants who, unable to endure their impoverished life anymore, had turned to Taiping-dao, the Doctrine of Peace.

Commoners' rebellion is like grass: trodden, yet rise again.
Their heads are like a chicken's: strangled, yet crow again.
No need to fear the officials.

려워했다. 그 눈동자 속의 아직 꺼지지 않은 불꽃의 이글거림을 마주하기 저어하였다. 언제나 오만하고 방자한 향도 가끔은 남편의 얼굴빛을 살펴 말을 꺼릴 지경이었다.

삭매의 가슴은 점차 싸늘하게 식어가고, 머리는 단순하고 뜨겁게 달구어졌다. 그 모든 환란이 오로지 땅, 땅, 땅을 차지하기 위한 쟁탈전으로 느껴졌다. 적과 아가 뒤엉킨 복마전이, 죽고 죽임의 피비린내 나는 살육이 결국은 빼앗은 땅 위에 자기의 깃발을 휘날리려는 음험한 도발이었다. 그럴수록 삭매의 마음은 이름도 없고 임자도 없는 땅, 아무도 소유하려 들지 않고 소유할 수도 없는 머나먼 땅으로 치달았다. 그 드넓은 광야, 삭막한 불모지가 바로 자신의 탯줄이 묻힌 고향이었다. 너무 멀리, 너무 오랫동안 떠나 있었을 뿐이었다.

옥문관과 양관 이서의 서역 제국은 이민족의 땅이었다. 나라의 기강이 확고할 시절, 서역은 모피와 모직물, 향료와 구슬 따위의 물품들로 풍요와 사치를 제공하는 지역이었다. 한(漢)은 이에 도호(都護)를 설립하여 얼굴빛깔과 말이 저마다 다른 무수한 이종족들을 다스리고

No need to slight the grass roots.

This wanderers' song kept ringing in Sakmae's ears, sung by those who had been forced off their land by the fear of floods, droughts, locust infestations, and earthquakes, combined with compulsory labor, diseases, and starvation. Remembering the mountains of dead bodies of those slaughtered in the bloody revenge, Sakmae gnashed his teeth with indignation. He could never be certain that the same would not occur again in the future. Then it would be his duty to pick up the sword and spear once again to massacre innocent people. In the same way as he had lived all his life, he would not hesitate to fight and fight against the poor peasants. And he would see grain and treasure in his storehouses amassed as high as the mounds of heads fallen at the sweeps of his half-moon sword.

Sakmae as a warrior was unswerving in his obedience and loyalty to his lord—but he could not quell the anguish in his heart. Try as he might, he only grew more reticent. His dignified appearance, weathered by the passage of the tempestuous times, and shrouded in silent solitude, kept others from approaching him. Everyone dreaded to be in

소통하였다. 바로 그 땅으로, 삭매에게 가라 하였다. 때마침 서역은 흉노의 침입으로 어수선하였다. 헌제 15년, 또한 건안(建安) 9년, 삭매는 서른여덟의 나이로 서역 정벌의 어명을 받았다. 환관 조등의 손자, 초 사람 조조가 헌제를 그의 땅 허현(許縣)에 맞아들여 "천자를 옹위하며 제후를 거느리는" 지위에 오른 지 9년째 되는 때였다.

그동안 영제가 죽고 소제(少帝)가 등극했다 폐출되며 헌제가 제위에 오르기까지 기나긴 할거의 전쟁이 치러졌다. 하진이 죽고 동탁이 죽고 이곽과 곽사가 서로를 죽이는 변란의 한가운데에서 단연 두각을 나타낸 조조는, 백골이 만 리에 낭자한 참상을 헤치고 보무도 당당히 지존의 자리에 올랐다. 삭매가 주군으로 충성을 맹세한 이는 분명 후한의 마지막 황제 헌제였다. 하지만 헌제의 명은 곧 조조의 명이었다. 조조의 명이라 하여도, 헌제의 명이었다. 삭매는 이미 원소와 조조의 관도(官渡) 전투에 참전한 바 있었다. 그때 조조는 군사력과 군량이 부족하고 후방이 안정되지 않긴 했지만 각개 격파와 기습, 군량 비축의 전술로 신속하게 원소의 군대

his presence. They saw still-unextinguished flames burning in his eyes and kept their distance. Even Xiang, normally arrogant and willful, would now and then hesitate to speak to her husband, after studying his countenance.

Sakmae's heart gradually turned cold and his head simple, yet hot. He thought that all the problems and disasters came from the struggles to possess more and more land. The pandemonium, with friends and enemies entangled in bloody battles and carnages, was caused by everyone's treacherous provocation so they could fly their flags in the conquered land. In agony, Sakmae's heart began to turn toward the nameless land far away that no one wanted and no one could own. That vast, desolate, barren plain was none other than his old home, his birthplace. He'd been too far away from home for much too long.

West of the Jade Gate, as well as the legations of Western countries, was the land belonging to the Western empires, the territories of foreign nations. While law and order were well enforced there, the Western countries had been the source of all kinds of abundance and lavishness—furs, wool, spices, beads, and so on.

를 궤멸하고, 마침내 중원을 통일하였다. 시대는 이미 그의 것이었다. 여씨 일가도 일찌감치 조조에게 투항함으로써 여건(呂虔)은 조조에게서 장교목수(將校牧守)라는 지위를 얻었다.

삭매는 서역 출병의 어명에 쾌재를 불렀다. 어명이란 거슬러 어길 수도 없으려니와, 한 손으로 화합의 악수를 하고 다른 한 손으로 경계의 칼을 휘두르는 군주 아래서 장수의 기개를 지키며 본분을 다하기란 낙타가 바늘구멍을 통과하는 일과 같이 어려웠다. 마침 그러한 때에, 끊임없는 전쟁의 시기를 틈타 북방에서 발호한 흉노의 호우(豪右)들과, 역(役)을 피하려 흉노 부락으로 도주한 한인들을 진압하기 위하여 삭매에게 서역 원정의 임무가 내린 것이다.

"정녕 가려오? 그곳은 다시 돌아오리란 약속 없이 떠나야 할 땅이라 아니 했소? 머나먼 이역, 땅의 끝이 아니오리까?"

아내 향이 삭매가 원정군의 수장으로 출병하게 되었다는 소식을 듣고 달려와 말하였다.

"땅의 끝이나, 새로운 하늘의 시작이오. 나 자신, 본디

The Han Dynasty had established a border administration to govern and communicate with the countless foreign races and tribes, with their different skin colors and languages. Now, Sakmae's heart told him to go to that land. At the time, that western region was troubled by the invasion of the Huns. In the 15th year of Emperor Xian (the ninth Jianan year), Sakmae received a royal command to subjugate the invaders. It was nine years after Cao Cao from the Kingdom of Chu, the grandson of Cao Teng the eunuch, had assumed the responsibility of "protecting the emperor and ruling the feudal lords" by inviting Emperor Xian to stay in his land of Xu Xian.

In the meantime, Emperor Yong had died and Emperor So had acceded to the throne. Until Emperor So was deposed and Emperor Xian was enthroned, a long series of wars among the rival warlords continued. After warlords like Ha Jin and Dong Zhuo died and I Guo and Guo Sa killed each other, Cao Cao stood out among all the remaining others, and in the end marched in proud array to the throne through the fields and fields of skeletons. It was Emperor Xian, the last emperor of the Later Han, to whom Sakmae pledged his loyalty.

모래 바람을 흡입하고 지붕 없는 집 안 나무 그늘 아래에서 별 떨기를 헤아리며 잠들던 태생이오. 그 사막의 언저리로 잠시 돌아가오. 그곳은 내 고향이니, 두려워할 것 없소."

"하지만 서역은 또한 죽음의 땅이니, 수많은 장사들이 오랑캐와 싸우다 사막 속에 뼈를 묻어 스러져간 곳이지 않아요? 지금이라도 늦지 않았으니 지병과 내환의 사유를 고하는 상소를 드리셔요. 중원 통일에 당신과 우리 집안의 공이 혁혁하니 천제도 간원을 물리치지 않으실 것이어요."

여전히 삭매의 마음을 헤아릴 줄 모르는 향은, 다시금 지금껏 확신하며 의지해 온 처세의 기술을 발휘하기에 골몰했다. 삭매는 향에게 자신의 마음속에 가득 찬 번민과 고뇌를 말할 수 없었다. 그 출구가 향에게는 황량한 열사의 땅으로만 보이는 서역을 향해 열려 있음 또한 말할 수 없었다. 삭매는 가볍게 한숨을 쉬며 말했다.

"대의멸친(大義滅親)이라 하여, 춘추 시대 석작은 나라를 위해 육친의 애정을 희생하여 친히 아들 석후의 목을 치려 하지 않았소? 나는 뼛속 깊이 변할 수 없는 장

Nevertheless, Emperor Xian's command was Cao Cao's; and Cao Cao's command was Emperor Xian's. Sakmae had already fought in the Guando battle between Yuan Shao and Cao Cao. At the time, despite the shortage of military strength and provisions and instability on the home front, Cao Cao had swiftly defeated Yuan Shao's army and unified the central fields of competition, using the tactics of divide and conquer, surprise attacks, and laying in emergency provisions. Time was already on his side. The Lu family had surrendered early to Cao Cao and was given by Cao Cao the position of the officer in command.

Sakmae jumped at the royal order of the westward military expedition. Royal orders were not to be disregarded; but in truth it was as difficult as a camel going through the eye of a needle to maintain a warrior's integrity and fulfill his duty under a lord who shook hands with one hand and brandished a warning sword with the other. So it happened that Sakmae was obliged to go on the expedition to subdue the powerful clans of the Huns, who arose in the north and took advantage of the endless wartime. Sakmae was also ordered to stop the Han people from joining the Hun settlements in

수요. 장수에겐 오직 마혁과시(馬革裹屍)가 영광일 뿐이오. 나라를 세운 마원이 말하길, 지금은 흉노와 오환이 항상 우리 북쪽을 침범하고 있다. 나는 청하여 이것을 치려고 한다. 남자로 태어난 몸, 이제 피의 들판에서 죽으려 한다. 말가죽으로 시체를 싸서 묻어주기를 바랄 뿐, 어찌 편하게 이불에 누워서 자식들 손에 싸여질 것인가, 하지 않았소? 당신의 내조지현(內助之賢)은 내가 갈 길로 가게 하는 것이오. 부디 아이들을 부탁하오."

그제야 향은 삭매의 결심이 단호하고 확고하다는 것을 깨닫고 설득하기를 포기했다. 그녀는 곧 얼굴에 가득 차 있던 수심의 빛을 지우고 냉정하게 말했다.

"그러시구려. 당신이 원하는 길을 떠난다는 데야 형처돈아(荊妻豚兒)는 모두 잊고 부디 어명을 받들어 충성하소서!"

초라한 처와 돼지의 자식을 잊고 원하는 대로 대의에 충실하라는 향의 말은 듣기에 따라 명분을 좇아 실리를 포기하는 삭매의 평소 행태에 대한 노골적인 비아냥거림인 듯도 하였다. 실로 자신의 아내를 겸손하게 낮추어 형처(荊妻)라 소개하는 관리 양홍의 소문을 듣고, 향

order to escape their duty of military service.

"Are you really leaving? Did I not I tell you that this expedition holds no promise of returning home. it is a faraway, alien land, the edge of the Empire, isn't it?" said his wife, who rushed to him upon hearing the news that he was appointed as head of the expeditionary army.

"Yes, it is the edge of the Empire, but it is also the beginning of new heavens. As for me, I used to breathe the sandy air and fall asleep under a tree or in a roofless house, counting the stars. I am going back to that edge of the desert to stay awhile. That place is my home, so there is nothing to worry about."

"But the western end is also the land of the dead, where countless men of strength fought against barbarians, only to have their bones buried in the desert. It's not too late. Please, make a petition to the Emperor saying that you have a chronic illness and troubles at home. With your and our family's distinguished services, unifying the central fields of competition, the Emperor will not refuse your entreaty."

Still unable to appreciate Sakmae's heart, Xiang once more was bent on exerting her art of worldly

은 그의 아내가 꽂았다는 가시나무 비녀의 이야기를 한동안 비웃어 마지않았다. 나라가 무너진다는 것이 바로 그러하였다. 어제의 미덕이 오늘의 비웃음을 사고, 어제의 악덕이 오늘의 칭송을 받는.

삭매는 이십 여 년의 고단한 청춘이 묻혀 있는 낙양을 떠나 돈황으로 향했다. 그리고 돈황에서 정예군 천 명을 이끌고 보무도 당당히 옥문관(玉門關)을 나섰다.

"병사여, 그대들은 어디로 가고 있는가? 이 길은 장건이 가고 반초(班超)가 간 바로 그 길이다! 반고(班固)의 제(弟) 반초는 흉노가 자주 변경에 침범하여 주민을 살상하는 바람에 가곡관의 성문을 밤낮없이 폐쇄하고 있다는 소문을 듣고, 글을 쓰던 붓을 분연히 집어던지고 스스로 무장을 갖추어 원정군에 가담하였다. 그는 대장부로 태어나 마땅히 장건을 본받아 이역에 공을 세우는 것이 떳떳한 일이거늘, 어찌 편안히 집에 앉아 필연을 벗하는 것만으로 일을 삼겠는가 하였다. 백여 년 전 장수의 피가 지금도 뜨겁게 느껴지지 않는가? 바로 우리의 핏줄기 속에서 들끓는다! 제아무리 흉노의 무리가 흉포하다 하여도 천제의 어명을 받잡은 우리에 감히 맞

wisdom that she had always relied on. Sakmae couldn't tell Xiang about the anguish and suffering that filled his heart. Nor could he tell her that, for him, the relief lay in the west, which she saw only as a desolate land of hot sand. Sakmae let out a brief sigh, and said:

"You know the old teaching, 'fulfillment of one's duty before the well-being of his family,' do you not? Sok Chak himself in the era of Chunchu decided to behead his son Sok Hu for the sake of his country. I am a warrior through and through. For a warrior, the only honor is 'getting his corpse shrouded in horse hide.' The founding father Ma Won once said, 'Now, the Huns and the Wuwans keep invading us from the north. I will take it on myself to defeat them. Born as a man, I am willing to die in the field of blood. All I am asking is to bury my body shrouded in horse hide. I refuse to die in bed and be shrouded at the hands of my children.' The wise way for you to help me now is to let me go where I am supposed to go. Please, take care of our children."

Only then did Xiang realize that Sakmae's resolution was firm and gave up persuading him. With the expression of sadness on her face fading instantly,

서 목숨을 보존할 수 있을까? 가자! 병사들이여! 북을 쳐라! 징을 울려라! 이제, 출정이다!"

삭매의 노호와 같은 웅변에 사기충천한 병사들은 칼과 창을 드높여 답했다. 돈황에서 나고 자라 용병이 된 그들에게는 두 명의 영웅이 있었으니, 장사 삭반(索班)과 장군 삭매였다. 집채만 한 바위들을 부딪쳐 부싯돌 삼았다는 전설의 장사 삭반은 바로 아이태산(阿爾泰山)에 잔류하고 있던 흉노에 의해 살해당했으니, 이번의 정벌은 그에 대한 돈황 청년들의 복수전이기도 했다.

살아 있는 전설 삭매는 두려움과 함께 크나큰 동경의 대상이었다. 변방의 우울과 소외를 앓고 있는 청년들에게 삭매는 곧 낙양, 그 번화한 세상에 대한 꿈이었다. 단 한 번만이라도 세상의 중심에 곧추섰다 고꾸라지고 싶었다. 그것만이 진정 장수답게 사는 길이었다. 부질없이 긴 목숨을 견디기엔 그들의 피가 너무 뜨거웠다. 그리하여 돈황의 병사들은 앞다투어 삭매의 원정군을 자원했다. 사막의 언저리에서 살아온 그들은 누구보다 불모의 땅의 가혹함을 잘 알고 있었다. 하지만 죽음의 위험을 불사함이 곧 새로운 삶의 기회였다. 삭매의 서역

she said coldly:

"Do as you wish. Well, if you insist on leaving ...May you stay loyal to the Emperor and forget all about your humble wife and sons!"

Depending on how one took it, Xiang's last words might have been said in outright sarcasm about Sakmae's lifelong mind-set of sacrificing practical benefits for the sake of moral obligations. In fact, on hearing the rumor that Official Yang Hong had introduced his wife using the humble expression "wife with a brier hairpin," Xiang had kept laughing for quite a while at the story of the brier hairpin that Yang Hong's wife wore in her hair. That is how a country collapses: yesterday's virtue is today's laughingstock, and yesterday's vice turns into something to be praised.

Sakmae left Luoyang, where the twenty-odd years of his youth were buried, for Dunhuang. And once in Dunhuang, he led a thousand elite soldiers to march out through the Jade Gate in a proud array.

"Soldiers, do you know where you are? This is the road on which Chang Gon and Ban Chao walked!" Sakmae cried out. "When Ban Chao, Ban Go's brother, heard that the castle gate of Jiayu-

원정이 성공한다면 그들은 함께 낙양에 입성할 것이다. 그리고 또 다른 삭매가 되어 낙양의 세련되고 나긋한 처자들의 마음을 흔들고, 천제의 깃발 아래 세상을 움직이게 될 것이다. 그리 품은 각각의 소망으로 천여 명 정예군의 사기는 하늘을 찌를 듯 드높았다.

사막은 가없이 뜨겁고 멀었다. 모래 바람에 쓸린 둔덕들은 짐승처럼 살아 꿈틀거렸다. 그 불동산을 팍팍한 다리로 거슬러 오르면, 어느덧 눈앞에는 지나온 모든 언덕 굽이들이 다시 앞질러 펼쳐져 있었다. 태양은 이글거리며 수만 개의 날선 화살을 땅으로 내리꽂고 있었다. 부서진 땅의 파편들이 서로 타협할 수 없는 모래알로 서걱거렸다. 그곳에서는 아무도 땅에 대해, 날씨에 대해, 길에 대해 말하지 않았다. 뜨거움에 이어진 뜨거움을 헤쳐, 길 없는 길을 한정 없이 좇을 따름이었다. 인간의 침묵, 그리하여 얻어진 한없는 정적이었다. 사막을 지키는 병졸과도 같은 뱀과 전갈과 도마뱀도 뜨거운 햇살 아래 잠복 중이었다. 그들조차 새벽과 저녁 한밤중에만 모습을 드러낸다. 흑색의 자갈로 뒤덮인 머나먼 지평선 이편에, 살아 지껄이는 것 아무도 없었다.

guan had to be locked day and night because the Huns often invaded the border and killed many villagers, he resolutely threw down his writing brush, armed himself, and joined the expeditionary troops. He said, 'Born as a man, it is an honor to render distinguished service in the alien land, following in Chang Gon's footsteps. How can I possibly sit comfortably at home, engaged only in literary work?' Don't you feel the hot blood of that warrior who lived some hundred years ago? Now, his blood is boiling in our veins! However ferocious the Huns may be, can they be spared their lives if they dare to fight against us, the army ready to carry out the Emperor's command? Forward, soldiers! Beat the drums! Strike the gongs! To war!"

Sakmae's roaring oration made the soldiers' morale soar to the skies and they responded vigorously, raising high their swords and spears. Born and bred in Dunhuang, the mercenary soldiers had two heroes to look up to: Sak Ban, a man of Herculean strength, and General Sakmae. According to legend, Sak Ban had smashed two rocks as big as a house against each other to use them as flints. To his people's chagrin, however, Sak Ban was killed by the Hun remnants hiding in Aitae Mountain. In a

선두에 선 삭매는 이따금 눈을 들어, 대지 저편을 병풍처럼 둘러싼 회황색 연봉들을 아득히 바라보았다. 그 바위산의 이마에는 들끓는 사막의 더위에도 결코 자세를 흐트러뜨리지 않는 만년설이 하얗게 흐르고 있을 터이다. 그 지맥이 바로 천산산맥, 흉노들은 그를 가리켜 하늘 산맥이라 부른다 하였다. 하늘, 닿을 수 없는 그곳은 홀연하였다. 막막한 외로움과 고독은 어리석은 인간의 것일 뿐, 언제까지나 정복될 수 없는 하늘 산의 위용은 무상하고 무심할 따름이었다. 그 아래에서 시간이, 기억이, 상념들이 점차로 아슴하게 사라져갔다. 존재까지도, 먼지처럼.

"대단한 지형이군요. 마치 망망대해를 표류하는 것 같습니다. 아이의 공깃돌 같던 바위가 다가서니 집채만 하고, 먼 바다 파고를 헤아릴 수 없듯 어느덧 지평선은 가파른 굴곡이외다. 오르고 내림에 따라 넓고 좁혀지는 시야가 눈속임인 양 극단에 이르니, 매복 작전에 매우 적합한 곳인 듯합니다."

이따금 넋을 놓은 듯 아득해지는 삭매를 일깨우는 것은 언제나 부관 장(張)이었다. 그는 해안 지방에서 치안

sense, for the young men of Dunhuang, the expedition was an opportunity to carry out their revenge.

Sakmae, a living legend, was the object of their fear and admiration at the same time. To the young men of Dunhuang, suffering from the gloom and isolation of the remote regions, he represented their dream of entering Luoyang, the bustling and thriving world. Even if it was only once in their lifetimes, they wished they could experience the center of the world. They believed that was the only way of life for a warrior worthy of the name. Their blood ran too hot to live a long but useless life. Therefore, the soldiers in Dunhuang rushed to join Sakmae's expeditionary army. Having lived on the edge of the desert, they knew better than anyone the cruelty of the barren land; but they also knew that risking their life was grabbing at a chance to start a new life. If Sakmae's expedition to the west succeeded, they would be able to enter Luoyang with the general. Then they would become like Sakmae, stirring up the hearts of the elegant and affable maidens in Luoyang, and be part of the force to control the world under the Emperor's flag. With that vision in their hearts, the thousand

관 위(尉)의 벼슬을 지내던 이로 이역에 대한 동경을 실현코자 삭매와 함께 서역 정벌에 나선 장수였다. 장은 보기 드물게 냉철한 지성으로 빛나는 자로, 광야에서의 초월적 거리 감각을 곧바로 매복 작전과 연관시켜 조언하였다. 지장과 용장의 결합 앞에 거칠 것이 없었다. 삭매의 부대는 날로 승승장구, 모래벌판을 휘저으며 흉노의 무리를 격퇴하였다.

그러한 어느 날, 사흘 밤낮을 꼬박 지속한 사막의 행군에 모두가 기진맥진하여 지쳐 있을 때였다. 사람도 동물도 뜨거운 대지와 건조한 공기에 시달리다 못해 창백해진 모습이 허깨비와 같았다. 병졸들의 수통은 벌써 비어 있었다. 삭매는 자신의 수통을, 탈진해 동료들에게 끌려오는 어린 병사에게 건네주었다. 감사를 바칠 경황도 없는 듯 병사는 허겁지겁 수통을 빨았다. 돌려받은 수통에 남아 있는 것은 채 한 모금도 안 되는 물이었다. 삭매는 서글픈 갈증을 침묵으로 참았다. 칼과 창에 의한 것보다 더 가혹한 죽음이 기다리고 있는 곳, 어쩌면 죽음보다 더 고통스런 갈증이 인간의 오만을 다스리는 곳이 바로 사막이었다. 삭매는 고통스러웠으나 고

elite soldiers' spirits lifted sky-high.

The scorching desert continued without bounds. Its dunes, swept by the winds, squirmed like live animals. Each time the expedition climbed to the top of a fiery dune, dragging their weary feet, they would see before them an endless stretch of meandering dunes, as if they'd been overtaken by the ones they'd already passed. The sun kept shooting tens of thousands of sharp arrows, breaking up the land to smithereens. The grains of sand, unyielding with one another, were crunching under their feet. No one talked about the land, weather, or path. Through the ever-present heat, they merely trudged on and on along the untrodden path. All the humans were silent, making an abysmal stillness. The sentinels of the desert—snakes, scorpions, and lizards—were all in hiding to avoid the scalding sun, coming out only between nightfall and dawn. There was nothing alive to make any noise between the marching army and the faraway horizon, which seemed to be covered in black gravel.

In the lead Sakmae raised his eyes now and then to gaze far off at the chain of grey-yellow mountains, which surrounded the far side of the desert

통 속에 평온했다. 무념무상, 무감의 쾌감이었다. 만약 죽음이 이런 것이라면, 기꺼이 껴안아 그 앙상한 갈비뼈를 어루만지길 주저치 않을 것이다.

바로 그때, 온통 회색과 황색으로 갇힌 시야 저 끝에 문득 신기루인 양 초록이 비쳤다.

"마을이다! 물이다!"

앞서 가던 눈 밝은 정찰병이 달려오며 외쳤다. 병사들 모두가 고함을 지르며 뛰었다. 갈기까지 처진 채 곧 꺾일 듯한 다리를 본능적으로 내딛던 말들과 등짐에 겨운 낙타들까지 탄성을 올렸다. 사막 한가운데 푸른 샘이 돋는 마을이 거짓말처럼 그들의 앞에 나타났다. 그들은 양껏 물을 마시고 몸을 적셨다. 아샤 족의 마을 원주민들은 포도를 빚어 만든 술을 내고 양을 잡아 대접했다. 그들은 오랫동안 흉노의 횡포에 시달려온 터라, 원정군의 등장을 기뻐하며 환대했다. 그 밤은 늦도록 노래와 춤으로 흥건했다. 삭매도 오랜만에 갑옷의 끈을 늦추고 여독을 풀었다.

다음 날 새벽이었다. 삭매는 가벼운 차림으로 막사를 나와 마을 주변을 둘러보았다. 병사들은 모두 노독과

like a giant folding screen. He knew that the peaks of those rocky mountains were most likely covered with white ice-caps that would not budge even at the boiling heat of the desert. They were called the Tian Shan Mountains, or by the Huns, the Heavens Mountains. They looked like a mirage, unreachable. Profound loneliness and solitude seemed to belong only to the foolish human race; the majestic, unconquerable Heavens Mountains remained indifferent and timeless. Faced with such magnificence, the people's sense of time, memories, and thoughts all faded away. Even their very existence seemed to be swept away like dust in a gust of wind.

"Amazing terrain. It feels like we're adrift on a boundless sea," said Jang, Sakmae's adjutant general. "A rock that looks as small as a marble from a distance turns out to be as big as a house. As we also cannot fathom the height of the waves of faraway high seas, the horizon here surprises us by suddenly turning into a quick bend. The field of vision broadens and narrows abruptly as we climb up and down, as if to trick us. It is a perfect place to ambush one's enemy."

It was always Jang who brought Sakmae out of his occasional absentmindedness. He had been a

주독에 지쳐 쓰러져 잠들어 있는지 다른 막사는 기척 없이 고요했다. 부지런한 양치기 몇이 풀밭을 찾아 양 떼를 몰 뿐, 접대에 지친 마을 사람들의 모습도 보이지 않았다. 삭매는 하릴없이 이곳저곳을 거닐며 매어놓은 말과 원주민들의 파오를 살폈다. 이민족의 말로 겔이라 부르는 그들의 거처는 맨바닥의 흙 위에 양탄자를 깔고 천장에 원형의 구멍을 뚫어 창처럼 그것을 여닫아 환기를 하고 온도를 조절하는 구조였다.

그런데 엇비슷한 천막집이 연이은 부락지에서 유독 삭매의 눈을 파고드는 작은 파오 하나가 있었다. 일찌감치 기세를 뻗치는 햇살 아래 아슴아슴 빛나는 선명한 색깔들이 그 파오의 주변을 둘러싸고 있었다. 회색과 황색의 단조로움에 지친 눈에 그 색의 사치는 경이롭고도 신비하게 느껴졌다. 삭매의 발길이 끌리듯 절로 그곳에 닿았다.

꽃!

사막을 건너는 동안 지치도록 보아온 선인장이나 가시를 온몸에 곧추세운 낙타풀의 흰 꽃이 아니었다. 그처럼 생존에 필사적인 마른 꽃들이 아니되, 물기 헤픈

superintendent at the level of *ui* officer in the law-enforcement authorities in a coastal region before joining Sakmae's expeditionary army in order to fulfill his dream of traveling to alien lands. A man of extraordinary intelligence, Jang advised Sakmae on the possibility of taking advantage of the illusory sense of distance in that vast open space in planning ambush operations. The combination of a resourceful warrior and a brave general made the army invincible. As a result, Sakmae's army was victorious in every battle, defeating the Huns across the vast plain of sand.

One day, everyone was completely exhausted after marching through the desert nonstop for three days and nights. Suffering so much from the heat and dry air, both the humans and animals had turned so pale they looked like phantoms. The soldiers' water bottles were empty. Sakmae gave his water bottle to a young soldier worn out and carried by his fellow soldiers. The soldier was in no state to thank Sakmae; he just took the bottle and began gulping down the water. When Sakmae got his bottle back, there was less than a mouthful left in it. Sakmae endured his thirst in silence. A crueler death than being killed with a sword or spear was

남방의 휘황하나 허황된 꽃들처럼 나른하지도 않았다. 파오를 둘러싸고 오롯이 피어난 그것들에겐 긴장이 있었다. 그 아슬하게 내린 뿌리에는 열매를 맺으려는 보존의 본성과 삭막한 자연이 대치하는 갈등이 있었다. 그리하여 그토록 아름다웠을 것이다. 있을 곳 아닌 데 있어, 아름답기로 다하기보다 차라리 아픔처럼 싸한.

제비꽃의 자매인 듯 더욱 아련한 자색 꽃과, 민들레처럼 낮은 키에 꽃잎이 조금 넓은 노란 꽃이었다. 물기를 머금어 생생한 그것들은 마치 한낮에 피어난 별꽃 같았다. 삭매는 조심스레 다가가 여린 꽃잎을 어루만졌다. 방울져 맺혀 있는 물기는 이슬이 아니라 누군가 머물러 간 사람의 흔적 같았다. 누굴까? 사막 한가운데에서 꽃을 기르는 이는. 누구라도 어지간히 부지런하고 강단 있지 않으면 안 될 터이다. 푸른 물이 돋는 샘도 언제까지 영원하진 않는다. 우물도 언젠가 마를 것이고, 잠시 축복을 누렸던 부족의 무리는 새로운 샘과 먹을거리를 찾아 길을 떠나야 할 것이다. 그러하기에 물로 누리는 모든 사치는 죄악이었다. 그런 비난을 감수하며 새벽 일찍 샘을 길어 꽃을 기르는 이는 과연 누구일까?

perishing while waiting for them in the desert. Perhaps it was a place where human arrogance is subdued by thirst, which can be more painful than death itself. Sakmae was in pain, but he somehow felt peaceful. He felt the pleasure of freedom from all worldly thoughts and emotions. If death comes to me like this, he thought, I'm willing to embrace it and stroke its dried-up bones.

Just then, they spotted far away something green among the usual gray and yellow that filled their field of vision.

"A village! Water!" yelled one of the quick-sighted scouts who'd gone ahead of them and was running back.

All the soldiers began to run, letting out shouts of joy. Even the horses, which had been trudging wearily out of sheer instinct, with their manes hanging limply and legs about to fold, and the camels, which had barely persevered with the heavy burdens on their backs, also neighed and brayed happily. Before their eyes, in the middle of the desert, a village magically appeared blessed with a spring. They drank their fill and washed themselves. The native people of the Asha tribe served them wine and mutton. Having suffered

그때 마침 파오에서 작은 물체 하나가 불쑥 튀어나오더니 삭매 앞에 오뚝 섰다.

"너, 너냐? 네가 이 꽃의 주인이냐?"

남의 집을 기웃거린 처지에 민망해 할 겨를도 없이 삭매는 얼결에 마음속에 담았던 의문을 불쑥 털어놓았다. 하지만 상대는 마치 책망이라도 당한 듯 대답도 않고 고개를 푹 숙이고 있다가, 불현듯 뒷걸음쳐 숲 사이로 도망갔다. 뒤쫓아 갈 염도 내지 못하고 삭매는 맥없이 그를 놓쳤다. 남은 것은 찰나의 인상, 노루처럼 가늘고 긴 다리와 검은 눈썹 아래 빛나던 초록 어린 갈색 눈뿐이었다. 나이를 어림할 수 없었다. 소년인지 소녀인지도 알 수 없었다. 하지만 삭매의 가슴은 예리한 칼날이 스친 듯 쓰라림으로 옥죄어 들었다. 수많은 전투에 참전해 사선을 넘나들면서도 단 한 번 느껴보지 못한 덴 듯 뜨겁고 저릿한 감정이었다. 삭매는 스스로를 해명할 수 없는 당혹감에 사로잡힌 채 자줏빛 꽃 한 송이를 꺾어들고 자신의 막사로 돌아왔다.

침상에 놓인 꽃이 시들어 갈 무렵, 삭매는 내심 고대하였던 우연에 맞닥뜨렸다. 바로 눈앞에서 놓쳐버린 노

greatly from the tyranny of the Huns for a long time, the villagers welcomed the expeditionary army wholeheartedly. Songs and dances continued until late at night. Sakmae also loosened his armor strings and relaxed after a long and harsh expedition.

At dawn, Sakmae, lightly dressed, left his quarters in the camp to take a look around the village. The rest of the camp was quiet, without a stir. Exhausted and drunk, the soldiers seemed to be fast asleep. Except for a few diligent shepherds leading their flocks of sheep to the grazing land, he didn't see any of the villagers either, who must have been tired from attending on the soldiers. Sakmae wandered here and there, checking on the tethered horses and the *bao* transportable homes, which were called *ger* by the villagers. Inside a *bao* was floored with rugs spread on the ground and had a ventilating window in the ceiling that could be opened and closed to maintain a comfortable temperature.

Among the rows of similar-looking *bao* houses in the settlement, one small *bao* caught Sakmae's eye. The foot of the house was surrounded by vivid colors glinting under the sunlight, which was al-

루였다. 노루처럼 날렵한 몸매에 묘묘한 눈빛이 별꽃 같은 소녀였다. 삭매는 단번에 그녀를 알아보았다. 소녀도 삭매를 알아보았는지 갑옷을 입고 칼을 찬 수장의 모습에 휘둥그레진 두 눈을 이내 바닥으로 내리깔아버렸다.

"물엿 좀 사셔요! 저희가 직접 고아 만든 물엿이에요. 아주 달고 맛나요!"

입술을 깨물고 선 소녀를 대신하여 동행한 소년 아이가 삭매를 졸랐다. 그들이 들고 온 광주리에는 엿기름을 끓여 졸인 이(飴)와 새고기를 말린 거(腒) 따위의 먹거리가 들어 있었다. 삭매는 흥정도 없이 그들의 광주리를 통째로 샀다. 그리고 좋아라 달려 나간 소년을 뒤따라 휘장을 벗어나려던 소녀의 가는 팔목을 붙잡아 세웠다.

"다시, 올 수 있겠지? 해가 지면 널, 기다리고 있으마."

다음 날이면 부대는 다시금 이동을 해야 했다. 일거부불귀(一去復不歸), 한 번 떠나면 다시 돌아오기를 기약할 수 없는 길이었다. 삭매는 언제나처럼 드러내어 변함없는 태도로 하루의 책무를 수행했지만, 작전 회의를 하

ready vigorous even early in the morning. To his eyes, tired of looking at gray and dull yellow for so long, indulgence in these brilliant colors was miraculous and mysterious. Sakmae's feet were drawn to the *bao*.

Flowers!

They were neither the cactuses nor the white flowers of thorny camel shrubs (*Cymbopogon schoenanthus*) that he'd seen all through his expedition across the desert so that he'd got weary of them. The flowers around the *bao* were neither the kind that were desperate for water, nor the southern, overly watered ones that were gorgeous yet too gaudy and languid. There was a kind of tenseness in the flowers blooming quietly and detachedly around that *bao*. In their roots, shallow but determined, was a conflict between the instinct of self-preservation, by bearing fruit and seeds, and their barren environment. Perhaps that was why they looked so beautiful. Growing where they were not supposed to gave them a look of poignancy, rather than of supreme beauty.

There were purple flowers that seemed to be in the violet family and bright golden ones that were as short-stemmed as, but with slightly larger petals

고 대열을 점검하는 중에도 문득문득 아득해지는 스스로를 느꼈다. 어린 날, 풀숲에 흘러 들어간 구슬을 찾지 못해 조바심쳤던 일이 생각났다. 어딘가에서 분명히 빛나고 있을 그것, 눈앞에서 놓쳐버리고도 다시 찾지 못한 그것 때문에 어린 마음을 한동안 앓았다. 오직 그 자신에게만 의미가 있는 갈망, 비밀스러운 조바심이었다. 하지만 삭매는 잃어버린 구슬과 달리 그녀는 반드시 그의 앞에 다시 나타나리라 믿고 있었다. 막연하지만, 뿌리칠 수 없는 확신이었다.

밤이 깊어 보초를 서는 병졸이 졸음에 겨워 눈을 비빌 때쯤, 삭매의 막사로 그녀가 찾아들었다. 삭매는 기쁜 빛도 없이 담담히 그녀를 맞았다.

"왜 저를 부르셨나요?"

소녀는 부질없는 질문으로 입을 열었다. 여린 얼굴 생김에 걸맞지 않게 목소리는 낮고 부드러웠다. 아침에 보았을 때와 달리 불빛 아래 가죽옷을 죄어 입은 모습은 숙성한 여인의 향기를 물씬 풍겼다. 그러면서도 소녀는 요염하다기보다 그 분위기가 미소년처럼 서늘했다. 삭매는 다시금 자신의 입 안을 바싹 태우는 불덩이

than, dandelions. Their vivid, bedewed petals twinkled like stars that had come out in broad daylight. Sakmae walked up to them and carefully stroked their delicate petals. Then, he thought the dewdrops on them might not be dewdrops after all. Perhaps somebody has just watered them. Who could that be, who is growing flowers in the middle of this desert? Whoever it is must be someone of diligence and tenacity. The spring won't last forever. When it dries up someday, the people of the tribe, who have enjoyed their blessing for a while, will have to leave the place to look for a new spring and food. Therefore, all water-related extravagances are considered vice. Who then can fetch water from the spring early in the morning to keep these flowers alive, while having to put up with all the censure?

Just then, a small person bounded out of the *bao* and came to a halt in front of him.

"Who are you? Are you the owner of these flowers?" Sakmae asked.

In no frame of mind to feel apologetic for snooping around someone else's home, he blurted out the question. But the person kept silent, head bowed for a moment, and then quickly stepped

를 마른 목젖 너머로 꿀꺽 삼켰다.

“이름이 무엇이냐?”

“자미(紫薇)입니다.”

“자미? 맨드라미를 말함이냐?”

“네. 소녀는 탯줄도 끊기기 전에 어미를 잃었습니다. 그때 어미가 왈칵 토해 놓은 피가 한 무더기의 맨드라미 같다고 하여, 아비는 소녀의 이름을 자미라 지었답니다.”

“그럼 아침에 동행했던 소년 아이는 아비가 취배하여 얻은 이복동생이냐?”

“함께 왔던 아이는 외사촌입니다. 아비는 핏덩이의 이름만 지어놓고 모래 언덕 저편으로 떠나버렸습니다. 그는 방랑자이자 순례자였습니다.”

상실의 기억을 말하는 자미의 얼굴에 잠시 우울한 그늘이 드리워졌다. 하지만 그 목소리에는 미동이 없었고, 입가에 비틀린 미소는 여전히 가까운 듯 먼 달빛처럼 묘연했다.

“나이는 몇이냐?”

“달이 기울어 지난 삭망에 꼬박 열여섯 해를 채웠습

backward and ran away through the woods, perhaps having taken his question as a reproach.

Dumbstruck, all Sakmae could do was just stand there and watch the person disappear. Brief as the encounter had been, he was impressed by the long slender legs, like those of a roe deer, and the greenish-brown eyes twinkling under dark eyebrows. He couldn't tell the person's age—he didn't even know if it was a boy or a girl. Nonetheless, Sakmae felt his heart tightening with an ache, as if it had been grazed against a sharp knife. He had never felt anything like it before, even while face to face with death in countless battles. It was a sensation at once scalding and numbing. Overwhelmed by his inexplicable confusion, Sakmae returned to his quarters with a purple flower in his hand.

By the time the flower had begun to wither at the head of his bed, Sakmae had another encounter, as he'd been secretly hoping to, with the "roe deer" that had run away under his eyes. It was a girl, as slender as a deer, with eyes twinkling like the chickweed with its star-shaped flowers. Sakmae recognized her right away. Perhaps the girl also recognized him, since at the sight of him in his commander's armor and sword, she looked at Sak-

니다."

"열여섯, 파과지년(破瓜之年)이라."

자미는 삭매의 장녀인 낭희(朗姬)와 동갑이었다. 하지만 삭매의 마음은 묵직한 중량감으로 다가오는 가족의 기억과 도덕의 굴레를 지나치듯 벗어나, 열여섯의 소녀를 더없이 아름답게 노래한 진나라 손작의 시 〈정인벽옥가〉에 닿았다.

푸른 구슬 참외를 깰 때에
님은 사랑을 못 견디어 넘어져 궁굴었네
님에게 감격하여 부끄러워 붉히지도 않고
몸을 돌려 님의 품에 안겼네

자미는 삭매를 거부하지 않았다. 이름과 나이를 물은 것만으로, 더 이상 아무 궁금증도 없는 듯 대화가 끊겼다. 자미는 부끄러움으로 눈을 피하거나 몸을 가리지 않았다. 달빛 아래 모래 들판처럼 은백색으로 눈부신 알몸을 드러내고도 두려움 없는 마알간 눈으로 삭매를 또렷이 바라보았다. 모든 것을 이미 아는 듯, 어쩌면 만

mae with her eyes wide open, only to cast them down quickly.

"Would you like to buy some starch syrup? We made it ourselves. It's really sweet and delicious!" asked a boy accompanying her, on behalf of the girl who stood there biting her lip. In their basket were malt extract, dried bird meat, and other foods. Sakmae bought the whole basketful without asking how much they were. The boy was so happy that he ran out of the curtain screen alone, leaving the girl behind. When she was about to follow the boy, Sakmae held her by the slender wrist.

"You will come again, won't you? At nightfall...I will be waiting for you."

The next day, the army would be back on the move again. There was no promise of return once they left the village. Throughout the day, Sakmae carried out his tasks, trying to be as calm as normal; but he could not help feeling dazed now and then while presiding over a council of war and inspecting the battle formation. He was reminded of a marble that he had lost as a child. After the marble disappeared into a thicket, he desperately looked for it, in vain. He had his heart broken over the marble he had lost right under his nose, which

나기 전부터 알아온 듯 낯섦이 없었다. 그 나이를 뛰어 넘은 담대함이 천박한 교태로 보이지 않고, 되레 준비하여 기다린 것을 맞아들이는 듯 자연스러웠다. 불혹지세를 코앞에 둔 삭매도 돌연히 휩쓸어온 강렬한 미혹에 포박당하길 주저하지 않았다. 오랜 불감이 무감무상으로 비워진 자리에, 자미의 존재가 고요히 들었다.

다음 날 마을을 출발해 다시금 사막을 행군하기 시작한 삭매의 부대에는 낯선 장수 하나가 끼어 있었다. 갑옷이 버거워 보이도록 길고 가는 팔다리에 앳된 얼굴을 지닌 소년 사병이었다. 삭매는 그를 자운(紫雲)이라 불렀다. 아샤 족 소년 중 유달리 기상이 호방하고 총명하여 이민족과의 통역을 위해 발탁한 자라 하였다. 하지만 그의 정체는 불분명하고 수상하기 그지없었다. 그는 별로 말이 없었으며, 삭매의 배려로 막사를 따로 썼다.

영원한 비밀은 없었다. 사나운 장수들의 눈을 오래 속이기란 애초에 틀린 일이었다. 한 사람, 두 사람의 입을 통해 행군 대열에 남장을 한 여자가 있다는 사실이 곧 모든 부대원에게 알려졌다. 돌연 군대의 내부는 미묘한 흥분으로 술렁거렸다. 혹간 이동 중 거쳐가는 마을에서

was shining somewhere in the thicket. The heart-ache lasted for quite a while, then turned into something tantalizing—a secret craving that was meaningful to him alone. However, Sakmae was convinced that, unlike the lost marble, the girl would come back to him. It was a groundless conviction, but an unshakable one.

Late at night, when the soldiers keeping sentinel were struggling with sleepiness, the girl came into Sakmae's quarters. Sakmae met her calmly, not showing a sign of happiness.

"What did you want to see me for?" the girl opened her mouth with the futile question. Unlike her delicate face, the tone of her voice was low and soft. She looked different from the girl he'd seen that morning. In the lamp light, her figure in the tightly-fitting leather clothes appeared to be much more mature. Yet she had an aura of a fair-faced boy, a coolness, rather than that of a sensual woman. Sakmae once more swallowed hard, his mouth parched as if there were a ball of fire in it.

"What is your name?"

"I'm Jami."

"Jami? It means 'cockscomb', doesn't it?"

"Yes, it does. I lost my mother even before my

호희(胡姬)들과 정분이 나거나 춘정을 감당 못 해 부녀자를 희롱하는 사고가 있기는 하였으나, 그것은 어디까지나 순간에 끝나는 일이었다. 장수들은 어느 땅에 뼈를 묻을지 알 수 없음과 마찬가지로 길 위에서 만났다 길 위에서 헤어지는 이별의 운명을 스스로 깨닫고 있었다. 그리하여 깊이 마음을 주지도, 오래 마음을 앓지도 않았다. 그런데 대열에 몰래 끼어든 여자라니! 그도 다름 아닌 장군 삭매의 여자라는 사실이 알려지자 장수들은 모두 경악을 금치 못했다.

산을 움직이고 물줄기의 흐름을 바꿀 듯한 장수였다. 숱한 전장에서 피로 목욕을 하며 뼈를 굵혀온 맹장이요 용장이었다. 침묵은 수심을 헤아릴 수 없는 강과 같고 분노는 용암이 흐르는 화산과 같았다. 그러한 영웅을 무너뜨린 여자, 스스로 금과옥조의 규율을 어기도록 만든 존재에 대해 모두의 호기심이 집중되었다. 하지만 누구도 그 여자에게 쉽게 접근하지 못했다. 자운의 주변에는 언제나 삭매의 그림자가 어른거렸다. 장수들 중에는 삭매의 눈을 정면으로 마주할 자가 아무도 없었다. 그만큼 삭매는 두려운 존재였다.

umbilical cord was severed. At the time of her death, my mother threw up blood. I was named Jami by my father because the blood looked like a bunch of cockscomb."

"If so, is the boy who came with you this morning your step-brother?"

"No. The boy is my cousin on my mother's side. Right after naming me, my father went away far beyond the sand dunes, leaving me behind. He was a wanderer, a pilgrim."

While she was talking about her lost parents, her face was briefly cast with a shadow of gloom. Nevertheless, her voice was steady and the twisted smile on her lips remained mysterious, like the moon appearing far and close at the same time.

"How old are you?"

"I turned sixteen last month."

"Sixteen, the age a girl comes to maturity..."

Jami was the same age as Sakmae's oldest daughter, Nang'hui. However, Sakmae's heart nimbly dodged the memory of his family and warded off the fetters of morality that had begun pressing hard upon him, and finally reached for "Green Jade Love Song," a poem composed by Son Jak of the Kingdom of Jin, which sang of a girl of sixteen

부하들에게 이 사태를 보고받은 장조차 분별심을 잃고 선불리 비평하기를 주저하였다. 장은 서둘러 이 문제를 불문에 부칠 것을 하명했다. 그리고 자신의 참전일지에 그때의 기록을 신음처럼 흘려 새겼다.

"수장이 병에 걸렸으니, 그 병명이 상사(相思)라. 외상은 없으나 내상이 치밀하여 판단이 흐리고 분간이 어렵도다. 상사지병에는 처방이 없어 스스로 낫기를 바랄 뿐이니, 오직 시간만을 의지하노라."

하지만 그 시각에도 삭매는 자신을 사로잡은 열병에 들끓고 있었다. 사랑을 묻는 자미 앞에서, 삭매는 무릎을 꿇고 말하였다.

"누구도 내게 사랑을 묻지 않았다. 묻지 않으니 답할 기회가 없었다. 묻지 않으니 스스로 답을 알려 하지도 않았다. 하지만 나는 유희로서의 사랑을 모르기에, 마음으로 여전히 동정(童貞)임을 주장하리라. 지금껏 단 한 번도 취첩하지 않았으니, 그것으로 내 절개와 신의를 증빙하리라. 오로지 생의 진정으로 너를 취하였으니, 너는 사랑을 묻기보다 삶과 죽음의 선택을 물어라. 사랑을 믿기보다는 차라리 내 목숨을 믿어라."

more beautifully than any other poem.

When green jade breaks a melon,
My lover falls over dazed in the grip of love.
Deeply moved by my lover, I blush not,
when losing myself in his embrace.

Jami did not refuse Sakmae. Having learned her name and age, he wanted to know nothing more. They stopped talking. Jami did not avert her eyes or cover herself out of shyness. Her skin shone silver-white, like the field of sand under the moonlight. She wasn't timid at all in her bare skin; rather, her clear eyes stared at Sakmae's. As if she understood everything, or as if she had known Sakmae even before their first encounter, she did not seem to feel awkward with him. Her boldness, uncommon at her young age, didn't look like a base coquetry, but was natural, as if she had been preparing for the moment. Although nearing forty, Sakmae was willing to be seized with such intense, unexpected seduction. He had long suffered from dissatisfaction, which had made his heart emotionless and thoughtless. But now Jami filled the void in his heart serenely.

삭매의 군대에 쫓긴 흉노는 천산산맥으로 퇴각해 있었다. 그들을 추격하기 위해서는 사막을 횡단해야 했다. 사주지로(絲綢之路, 실크로드)의 여정은 온통 뜨거움과 목마름으로 가득 차 있었다. 길목에는 군데군데 사막을 헤매다 죽은 대상들의 뼈가 허옇게 드러나 있었다. 마흔두 살의 반초를 따라 처음 흉노 토벌군으로 서역의 들판에 나섰던 병사들은 모두 서른 명, 그러나 만년에 반초를 따라 낙양에 돌아온 이들 중 원년의 부대원은 단 한 명도 없었다. 그들은 모두 지표도 없는 사막에서 홀연히 사라졌다. 그리하여 남의 열 마디를 한 마디로 하는 문장가 사마천은 사막을 건너기를 '착공'이라 일렀다. 끌로 구멍을 파들어 가듯, 집요한 고통과 피로를 감내할 일에 다름 아니라고.

이곳의 싸움은 오직 그 불의 지옥 한가운데에 오롯이 존재하는 생명수의 마을, 천산산맥의 만년설이 녹아서 흘러드는 물로 만들어진 기적 같은 공간에 대한 쟁탈전이었다. 사람과 사람이 싸우고, 사람과 자연이 싸우고, 자연은 스스로 이글대며 싸웠다. 하지만 욕망의 충족을 목적으로 하는 싸움이 아니라 오직 생존을 위한 그것이

The next day, the army left the village to resume its march through the desert—with a new recruit among them. It was a boy-soldier with such slender and long arms and legs that his armor seemed burdensome on him. Sakmae called him Ja'un. He was said to have been chosen among the boys of Asha tribe for his valiant spirit and cleverness, to help with their communication with the foreign tribes. Among the rest of the army, however, he was considered a dubious character with an uncertain identity. He was always quiet and given his own quarters by Sakmae.

Nothing can be kept secret forever. There was no chance of deceiving fierce warriors' eyes. Word quickly spread from one man to another that there was a woman in disguise among the marching soldiers, until the entire army heard of it. Suddenly, the army was buzzing with a strange excitement. Once in a while, in the villages they passed through, some soldiers became intimate with the women entertainers from the Middle East, or unable to control their carnal desire, got themselves in trouble by harassing some village women. But that kind of trouble did not last long. As soldiers in an expeditionary army, they had come to under-

었으니, 싸움의 종말은 죽음이라기보다 증발이었다. 바싹 오그라져 타들어 날아가버리는 삶.

삭매의 군대는 십 일간의 지옥 같은 행군 끝에 누란을 지났다. 그런데 그때부터 뜻밖의 일이 벌어졌다. 비가 내리기 시작한 것이다.

"괴이한 일이로다. 남쪽의 거센 비바람과 비구름도 험봉을 넘지 못해 스러지고, 북쪽에서 불어온 높새바람으로 습기 없는 열풍이 가득 찬 이 땅에 난데없는 비라니!"

삽시간에 물에 빠진 듯 흠뻑 젖은 군사들과 갈기를 늘어뜨린 말과 낙타를 바라보며 삭매가 중얼거렸다.

"아주 없던 일은 아니랍니다. 드문 경우이긴 하지만 이곳에도 폭우가 몰아치는 때가 있다 합니다. 걱정은 광활한 분지에 내린 빗물이 오로지 한곳으로만 몰리는 것입니다. 여기에 날씨의 이변이 겹쳐 천산의 만년설이 더운 열에 녹아 흐르면 걷잡을 수 없는 홍수가 일어난다 합니다. 졸지에 모래땅 위에 없던 강이 생긴답니다. 아니, 강이라기보다 건천이라 합지요. 홍수 때만 엄청난 양의 물이 순식간에 흘러가며 주변 모든 것을 삼켜

stand their fate of unexpected meetings and partings, the same way they never knew when and where their corpses would be buried. Therefore, they had learned not to get deeply involved with anyone or to suffer for long from heartache. So the idea of a woman who'd sneaked in the army was not even in their wildest imaginations! When they learned that it was the commander's woman, they were thunderstruck.

To them, Sakmae seemed a great warrior, strong-willed enough to move a mountain and change the path of a river. He was a veteran fighter and dauntless general who had been bathed in blood and had his bones clipped in countless battles. His silence was as unfathomable as the depths of the sea and his fury like a volcano spewing lava. And yet there was a woman among them who had defeated him—a woman who had made Sakmae break his army's unspoken rule. Their curiosity was focused on her; nevertheless, no one dared to approach her. They saw Sakmae's shadow around Ja'un at all times. There was no one who was able to look Sakmae straight in the eye, so much did they fear their commander.

Even Jang, when reported to about the situation,

버리는, 그를 일러 원주민들은 그무 강이라고 부르더군요."

"그무 강, 그무 강의 홍수라."

삭매는 장의 말을 되풀이하여 곱씹었다. 아무래도 더 이상의 전진은 불가능한 듯 보였다. 삭매는 긴급한 명령으로 서둘러 임시 주둔지를 확보하고 막사를 쳐 비를 피했다. 하지만 수그러들 줄 모르는 빗줄기는 두꺼운 천막을 뚫고 막사 안에까지 쳐들어왔다. 굵은 빗줄기가 가죽 천장을 두들기는 소리로 요란스럽던 그날 밤, 복잡한 심경으로 뒤척이던 삭매의 처소에 낯선 방문객들이 찾아왔다.

"저희는 화주(火州) 인근 구자국에서 온 상인들입니다. 근간에 천제의 정벌군이 흉노를 몰아내어 다시금 하서회랑을 자유로이 오가며 무역을 하게 되었습니다. 그 은혜에 감읍하는 심정으로 밤늦게 장군의 잠을 깨우는 무례를 저질렀습니다."

"그래, 너희가 긴히 할 말이란 무엇이냐?"

"다름이 아니오라 저희가 오늘 지나온 마을에 며칠 전부터 흉노의 대부대가 집결해 있다는 말씀을 전하고

was careful not to lose his wits and hastily criticize his superior. He ordered an immediate silence about the matter. Then he inscribed the affair in his journal, as if letting out a groan:

"The commander has fallen ill. It is lovesickness. There is no visible injury, but his heart seems to be seriously affected. He appears to be lost to all sound judgment and sense. Since there is no cure for lovesickness, I hope it cures itself. All I can rely on is the passage of time."

Even at the time, however, Sakmae was in the grip of fever. Before Jami, who asked him if he truly loved her, Sakmae kneeled down and said:

"No one has ever asked me if I love her, therefore I have had no chance to answer the question, or even to think over it myself. Since I have never experienced love just for amusement, I claim to be a virgin in the heart. I have never kept a mistress, which proves my integrity and faithfulness. You are the only true love of my life, so rather than asking me if I love you, you should ask if I wish to live or die. Instead of trusting my love, trust my life."

Chased by Sakmae's troops, the Huns had retreated to the Tian Shan Mountains. In order to pursue them, Sakmae's army had to traverse the

자 합니다."

"그래? 그들의 수는 대략 몇이냐?"

"그들의 부대는 눈으로 어림하여 대략 이천 명 남짓한 듯합니다. 부디 그들을 섬멸하시어 서역의 평화를 되찾아주소서."

삭매는 구자국 상인들에게 큰 포상을 내렸다. 그리고 그들이 떠나자마자 각 부대의 수장들을 소집해 긴급회의를 열었다. 삭매의 생각은 지금 곧바로 출전 명령을 내려 퇴각해 있는 흉노를 치자는 것이었다. 하지만 일부에서는 야밤에 호우 속의 강행군을 한다는 것이 무리라는 의견도 있었다. 천 명의 병사로 이천 명의 적을 공격한다는 것이 부담스러우니 일단 상황을 주시하자는 의견도 있었다. 하지만 삭매의 의지는 단호했다.

"적의 숫자가 아의 배에 이름을 두려워하기 이전에, 돌이켜 우리의 군대를 살펴보시오. 투편단류(投鞭斷流)라, 우리 군의 병력으로 하면 전원의 채찍을 양자강에 던져 넣기만 해도 그 흐름을 차단할 수가 있소. 우리는 어중이떠중이 군대가 아닌 정예군이요, 거듭된 승리의 경험으로 사기가 충천하오. 그에 비한다면 지금 적의

desert. The march along the Silk Road meant nothing but enduring the scorching heat and thirst day after day. Here and there along the road they saw the white bones of the caravans that had met their deaths while wandering through the desert.

Forty-two-year-old Ban Chao had led his army of thirty soldiers through the western plain to put down the Huns for the first time. When he returned to Luoyang late in life, however, there was not even one original member left in his army. They had all vanished like smoke in that disorienting desert. Thus, Sima Qian, the writer who could express in one succinct phrase what others needed ten to describe, called crossing the desert "launching a construction." He likened it to enduring the persistently painful and exhausting work of construction, like boring a hole with a chisel through a rocky mountain.

The battles in the desert were fought for one reason: to occupy a lone village, a miraculous space in the middle of that burning hell of a desert, blessed with life-giving water from the stream of icecaps of the Tian Shan Mountains. Humans fought against humans; humans waged war against nature; and nature was in a fierce battle against it-

상태는 곤수유분투(困獸猶奮鬪)요, 쫓기는 동물일수록 더욱 필사적인 법이오. 흉노는 오랜 옛날부터 초원을 중심으로 유목 생활을 해온 호전적인 민족이라, 뛰어난 기마술로 기습적인 공격과 도주에 능하다고 정평이 나 있소. 우리가 이곳에 머물러 있음이 적에게 노출된다면 그들은 반드시 반격해 올 것이오. 하지만 아직 적은 우리의 동태를 파악하지 못했으니 지금의 작전은 기습이 최선이오. 적은 자신들의 장기로 우리에게 당하리라곤 절대 예상치 못할 테요. 당장, 바로 이 순간에 출전할 일이오."

지(智)와 용(勇)을 겸비한 삭매의 거침없는 사자후 앞에 부장들은 더 이상 반대의 뜻을 피력하지 못했다. 그들은 명령에 따라 서둘러 군대를 집결하여 정비하였다.

"따르라! 병사들이여! 이미 젖은 몸을 가리지 마라! 선발제인(先發制人)이면 완승이리니, 잠에 취해 꿈에서라도 싸울 줄 모르는 적의 무리는 그대들의 창칼 앞에 가랑잎같이 쓸려가리라! 가자! 필생의 용자들이여!"

삭매의 우레와 같은 포효에 병사들은 사기충천하여 칼과 창을 드높였다. 쏟아지는 빗속에서도 발걸음은 거

self. However, the wars in the desert were not fought to satisfy greed, but only for survival. In that sense, the end of a war meant evaporation rather than death, that is, life shrank, burned, and evaporated.

Sakmae's troops passed Loulan after a hellish, ten-day march. Then came an unexpected turn of event: It began to rain.

"How strange it is! Rain! In this land swept by the hot, dry northerly wind, where even the mighty southerly wind and rain clouds are unable to climb over the towering, rugged mountains," Sakmae muttered to himself, watching the soldiers who'd gotten soaked through in an instant, as if they'd fallen into water, and the camels and horses with their wet manes hanging limply.

"They say it is not unheard of, though very rare; heavy rain does hit this place, too," Jang spoke. "The problem is the rainwater from all across this vast plain flows to only one spot. And, what is more, if an unusual change of weather occurs and melts the icecaps of the Tian Shan Mountains at the same time, there will be an uncontrollable flood. Then all of a sudden, a river may appear across this land of sand, they say. In fact, it is not a real river.

침없이 앞으로 내달았다. 회오란 가당치 않았다. 그들은 이미 전투를 생의 업으로 삼은 용병으로, 그들의 고뇌 없는 일상은 삶과 죽음이 교차되어 직조된 피륙과도 같았다.

하지만 전투의 의지로 충만한 삭매의 군대 앞에는 뜻밖의 난관이 기다리고 있었다. 흉노가 집결해 있다는 마을로 가는 길목을 거대한 물줄기가 가로막고 있는 것이었다.

"그무, 그무 강이외다!"

삭매의 곁에 있던 장이 비명처럼 외쳤다.

하루 종일 줄기차게 내린 비로 말미암아 불어 오른 강물은 싯누런 물살을 출렁이며 흘러가고 있었다. 굽이치는 물살은 망령들의 휘파람인 양 쉭쉭 위협적인 바람소리를 내었다. 물결 군데군데 어지럽게 휘도는 소용돌이는 강물에 실려온 부유물들을 거침없이 집어삼키고 있었다. 위험을 감지하는 본능에 사람보다 빠르고 솔직한 동물들이 놀라 앞발을 치켜세우며 울부짖었다. 미친 물살이었다. 광란의 강이었다.

노도의 기세로 군대를 몰아온 삭매도 예상 밖의 복병

It is a dry riverbed that gets filled only at the time of flood when an enormous amount of water flows through it, swallowing up everything in its course. I have heard the native people call it the Gu'mu River."

"Gu'mu. The flood of the Gu'mu River..."

Sakmae repeated Jang's words, chewing over them. Marching any farther seemed impossible. Sakmae gave an emergency order to secure a campground immediately and put up barracks, to shelter themselves from the rain. Nevertheless, the rain got heavier and even seeped into the barracks. That night, while the thick sheets of rain pounded noisily on the leather ceiling of the commander's quarters, some strangers visited Sakmae, who was tossing and turning with many thoughts.

"We are merchants from the land of Kucha near Huo Zhou. Lately, thanks to the expeditionary army of the Emperor, we were able to resume our trade, freely traveling west of the Hexihuilang. It is discourteous of us to wake you up so late at night, but since we are moved to tears by the mercy shown to us, we have come to offer our appreciation."

"So, what is it that you want to tell me?"

"We would like to tell you that in the village we passed through this morning, a great number of

에 적이 당황하였다. 강가는 허허벌판으로, 비를 피할 바위 동굴은커녕 나무 한 그루조차 없었다. 병사들도 우왕좌왕하며 어쩔 줄을 몰라 했다. 각 부대의 수장들이 모여 머리를 맞대었으나 묘안이 없었다. 그토록 강기슭에 몰리듯 집결한 채, 삭매의 부대는 한참 동안 대책 없이 비에 노출되어 있었다.

삭매는 어떤 명령도 내릴 수가 없었다. 이대로 돌아설 수는 없다는 생각만이 머릿속에서 웅웅대며 떠돌았다. 그때 말없이 싯누런 강물을 지켜보고만 서 있는 삭매에게 장이 다가와 말하였다.

“무릇 물은 불과 달라, 불은 인간의 손끝을 잠시의 뜨거움과 아픔으로 데워 위험을 경계하나, 물은 평시에 부드럽고 여린 알랑거림으로 인간을 미혹하여 위험을 스스로 숨기는 속성이 있습니다. 하지만 어찌 불의 위험을 물의 위험에 비견하리오? 제가 나고 자란 지방에서 물일로 연명하는 우민들 사이에는 하신(河神)의 비위를 맞추는 이 가지 저 가지의 비방들이 전합니다. 그중 하신의 노여움을 풀기 위한 비방이 있으니, 제가 감히 장군께 여쭐 수 있겠는지요?”

Hun soldiers have been staying for the last few days."

"Is that right? About how many are there?"

"It seemed roughly two thousand. Please, defeat them and bring peace back in the west."

Sakmae rewarded the Kucha merchants generously, and as soon as they left, he convened an emergency meeting with the heads of all units of his army. He wanted to launch an attack right away on the Huns in retreat. However, some of his unit heads thought marching through the heavy rain in the dark was unwise. Others thought that since it seemed difficult to attack two thousand troops with only one thousand, it would be better to wait. Nevertheless, Sakmae was resolute in carrying out his plan.

"Before we get discouraged just because the enemy outnumbers us, let us take a clear look at our own army. As in the expression 'throw in the whip, cut the current,' our army can block the flow of the Yangtze River simply by throwing in all of our whips. We are an elite army, not some rabble. And our soldiers are in high spirits thanks to our continuous victories. Compared to our army, the enemy has been cornered, so they are desperate and

위급한 상황에 걸맞지 않는 긴 사설이 미심쩍기는 하였으나, 삭매는 지푸라기라도 잡는 심정으로 장의 말을 채근하였다.

"그 비방이란 것이 대체 무엇이냐?"

장은 잠시 머뭇거리더니, 결심한 듯 낮고 빠르게 말하였다.

"제물이 필요합니다. 본디 계집의 업은 재봉이요 사내의 업은 요리라 하나, 그중 신묘한 양조(釀造)의 책무는 허여(許與)에 능통한 여인들만이 맡아 할 수 있으니, 술도 물로 만들어짐에 물은 여인과 가깝다 하나이다. 살아 있는 여인을 바쳐야만 합니다. 그래야만 하신의 노여움이 풀리고, 우리는 능히 흉노를 칠 수 있습니다."

하지만 인가라곤 찾아볼 수 없는 고립무원의 강기슭에서 여인이라니. 그러다 문득 삭매는 불꽃이 튀는 눈을 부릅뜨고 장을 사납게 노려보았다. 매사에 침착한 장조차 그 눈길을 마주할 수 없어 황급히 고개를 떨구었다. 여인이 아주 없는 것은 아니었다. 천 명 중의 단 한 사람, 남장을 한 채 대열의 후미를 따르고 있는 자미, 그녀였다.

unafraid, like animals being chased. The Huns are warlike people, nomads who have been weathered since ancient times by the harsh life on the vast grasslands. They are known for their horse-riding skill, surprise attacks and swift retreats. Once we are exposed to them while staying here, they most certainly will retaliate on us. However, since they have not yet figured out our whereabouts, an immediate surprise attack is the best strategy. They are not expecting to taste their own medicine under our surprise attack. Now is the time to go to war."

Confronted with this impassioned speech by Sakmae, a man of intelligence and bravery, the unit heads could no longer oppose their commander in chief. Following Sakmae's order, they marshaled their troops.

"Follow me, Soldiers! There is no point in covering up ourselves since we are already soaked! Forestalling them now will get us yet another victory. The enemy is deep in sleep and will not be able to fight back. They will be swept off by your swords and spears like dead leaves! Onward, warriors born brave!"

Sakmae's thunderous roars lifted the soldiers'

하지만 삭매는 장의 건의를 아예 듣지 못한 듯 답도 없이 무거운 침묵 속에 빠져들었다. 더 이상 아무도 삭매에게 말을 붙이지 못했다. 가없는 침묵을 빗줄기만이 소란스레 파고들었다. 다만 삭매의 입에서 새어나올 그 어떤 말을 기다리느라 고요해진 좌중에 의구심, 불안감, 호기심 어린 시선들이 바쁘게 오갈 뿐이었다. 돌아서 강물을 마주해 서 있는 삭매는 등 뒤로 꽂히는 그 수많은 눈길의 화살들을 고스란히 느끼고 있었다. 그러나 아픈 곳은 집요한 의혹에 시달리는 등판이 아니라 헤쳐 보일 수 없는 가슴속이었다. 가슴을 관통한 화살은 단 하나, 날카롭게, 하여 서늘하게 날아온 군중 속 자미의 시선이었다. 그녀를 볼 수는 없었다. 하지만 느낄 수는 있었다. 삭매의 가슴을 꿰뚫은 무혈의 관통상이 선명하게 그녀의 존재를 입증하고 있었다. 잠시 선택의 기로에서 흔들린 마음을 헤집어든, 그 내상은 치명적이었다. 삭매는 온몸을 울려오는 저린 아픔을 참느라 어금니를 악물었다. 그리고 잔인한 시선들 앞으로 돌아서서 소리쳤다.

"강가에 제단을 쌓아라! 하신에게 노여움을 풀어달라

spirit high. Raising their swords and spears, they dashed forward undaunted even in the pouring rain. They were mercenary soldiers, in the trade of lifelong warring; their days, tightly woven with crisscrossed life and death, allowed no anguish to seep in.

However, an unexpected obstacle was waiting for the army, bursting with fighting spirit. On the way to the village where the Huns were staying, an enormous stream of water blocked their march.

"Gu'mu, it is the Gu'mu River!" Jang yelled, like a scream, beside Sakmae.

The downpour that continued the whole day had swelled the stream with yellowish, muddy water. The wildly churning current made a threatening, wind-like noise, as if it were the whistling of departed souls. The dizzying whirlpools in the current were relentlessly swallowing up the floats, which were carried away by the river. Animals, trusting more readily and responding more swiftly to their instincts, were so startled they ramped, pawing the air and neighing loudly. It was a crazed flood of water, a river of sheer frenzy.

Sakmae, who had been leading the army with the force of a surging wave, was taken aback by the

는 간청의 기도를 올리겠다!"

서둘러 제단이 축조되고 급히 조달된 제물이 바쳐졌다. 삭매는 무릎을 꿇고 제단 앞에 엎드려 오랜 시간 기도를 올렸다. 정녕 물의 흐름과 파고를 관장하는 신령의 의지가 무엇인지 묻고자 했다. 죽음의 길, 돌아갈 수 없는 길을 헤쳐 거슬러온 인간들의 간절한 기원을 전달하고자 했다. 하지만 하신의 대답 대신 주어진 것은 더욱 거세게 몰아치는 빗줄기뿐이었다. 강물의 기세도 더욱 드높아 누런 흙탕물이 마침내 삭매의 꿇어앉은 무릎을 적셨다.

"장군! 강물이 제단을 삼켰습니다! 물러나십시오! 이럴수록 하신의 노여움이 더욱 커질 뿐입니다! 어서, 어서 여인을 그에게 보내십시오! 그녀의 희생이 아니고는 다른 방법이 없습니다!"

장이 가슴까지 차오른 물살에도 미동 없이 앉아 있던 삭매를 잡아끌며 외쳤다. 하지만 삭매는 여전히 답을 하지 않았다. 굳게 닫힌 입술은 완강한 침묵 속에 끓어오르는 상념을 간신히 삼키는 듯하였다. 그의 눈동자에는 어느덧 분노의 불꽃이 이글거리고 있었다. 화(火)로

unexpected ambush by the river. The riverside was a vast empty field without a tree, let alone a cave where they could take shelter from the rain. The soldiers were rushing around in confusion. The unit heads gathered to come up with a solution, all to no avail. Huddling together on the riverside, as if cornered, Sakmae's army had no choice but to wait for as long as it took, helplessly exposed to the torrential rain.

Although Sakmae was unable to give any order at all, his head kept echoing with the resolution that he refused to turn back. Then Jang approached Sakmae, who had been staring silently at the muddy river, and said:

"Fire warns us humans immediately by paining us with its heat. Water, on the other hand, charms us with its tender and delicate appearance, hiding its deadly threat behind it. As a matter of fact, the danger of fire is no match for that of water. The ignorant people of my home province, whose livelihood depends on the river, believe in secrets to humor the river god; one of them is to appease the river god's wrath. With your permission, I would like to tell you what that is."

Although suspicious of Jang's wordiness at a time

수(水)를 멸할 수 있다 한다면, 그는 눈이라도 도려 뽑아 오만하게 일렁이는 물살에 던져 넣을 듯하였다. 장은 그토록 생경하게 느껴지는 공포의 무게에 저절로 한 발 뒤로 물러섰다.

삭매는 갑자기 메어 찬 칼집에서 장검을 빼어들었다. 그리고 서슬 퍼런 칼날을 입에 물고 두터운 먹장구름으로 가득 덮인 하늘을 날카롭게 노려보았다. 이미 싸움은 시작된 듯하였다. 얼굴 위로 거세게 내리꽂히는 빗줄기에 아랑곳없이 삭매의 노기에 찬 시선은 꿰뚫을 듯 하늘을 향했다. 이윽고 삭매는 칼날 위에 얹힌 입술을 거두어 하늘을 흔들고 땅을 울리는 목소리로 외쳤다.

"부대 전원은 전투 대형으로! 이 괴변을 획책한 자의 정체는 신이 아니라 악마다! 악마에게 기도가 통할 리 없다. 어리석은 짓이다. 방도는 무력뿐이다. 우리의 막강한 힘으로 강물의 악마를 물리치리라!"

산을 무너뜨리는 기세로 우르릉 꽝꽝 몰아치는 물살의 굉음을 가르고, 천둥소리 같은 삭매의 목소리가 울려 퍼졌다. 병사들은 무기를 바투 쥐고 재빨리 대열을 정비했다. 때마침 놀란 듯 비는 그쳤지만, 강물의 기세

of crisis, Sakmae urged him to go on, like a drowning man grasping at a straw:

"What on earth is that secret?"

Jang hesitated for a moment, before he determinedly began to talk rapidly under his breath:

"We will need an offering. There is a saying that needlework is for women while cooking is for men. Nevertheless, the mysterious working of brewing is left in the hands of female masters, who are good at praising and soothing. It is said that since brewing is done with water, women are intimate with water. A live woman must be offered, and the river god will be appeased and we will be able to attack the Huns."

But where can I find a woman on this forsaken riverside far away from any villages? Sakmae thought. Then, he suddenly glared at Jang with a flaming fury in his wide-open eyes. Even Jang, a man of poise, dropped his eyes, unable to look Sakmae in the eye. It was not that they had no woman at hand. There was one, among the thousand men, following in the rear of the march files: Jami.

Nevertheless, Sakmae remained in heavy silence, as if he had never heard Jang's suggestion. No one dared to speak to Sakmae anymore. Only the vio-

는 오히려 더욱 거세어졌다.

“활을 쏴라!”

삭매의 명령에 따라 사수들은 일제히 강을 향해 활을 쐈다. 화살들이 포물선을 그리며 날아가 누런 용틀임을 하고 있는 강물의 둔중한 몸피에 푹푹 꽂혔다.

“돌격하라!”

보병들이 함성을 지르며 창을 앞세우고 강물을 향해 뛰어들었다. 그들의 거센 발걸음을 북돋우고자 징과 북이 요란스레 울렸다. 병사들은 강물 속에서 정신없이 칼과 창을 휘둘렀다. 명령을 내린 자나 명령에 복종하는 자나 가릴 것 없이 무언가에 사로잡힌 듯하였다. 익히 들어온 과거의 전사(戰史)에서 찾아볼 수 없는 자연과 인간의 기이한 대결이었다. 하지만 이미 시작된 싸움의 결말은 승리가 아니라면 패배뿐이었다. 병사들은 필사적으로 강물에 맞서 활을 쏘고 창칼을 휘둘렀다. 전투는 어둠이 깃들 때까지 계속되었다.

그들은 어둠을 보았다. 어둠 속에서 꿈틀거리는 강물을 보았다. 그것은 이미 강물이 아니라 악마였다. 전투를 지휘하는 삭매의 눈에도, 기력이 다하도록 맞서 싸

lent sheets of rain pummeled in the endless silence. The rest of them were waiting for Sakmae to break the silence, busily exchanging glances of suspicion, anxiety, and curiosity. Sakmae was facing the water, feeling the countless arrows of their staring eyes piercing his back. What really hurt, though, was not his back tortured by their persistent suspicion, but his heart that could never be opened to reveal what was inside. What had penetrated his heart was the sharp, bloodcurdling arrow of Jami's eyes staring at him among the crowd. Though he could not see her, he was able to feel her stare. The bloodless piercing wound undeniably proved her very existence, and was all the more deadly since it was inflicted upon his heart wavering in a dilemma. He gritted his teeth to endure the excruciating pain coursing through his entire body, and turned around to face the cruel eyes and roared:

"Build an altar by the river! I shall offer a prayer of appeal to the river god!"

The altar was built and an offering procured and presented in haste. Sakmae knelt down before the altar and prayed for a long time. He truly wanted to know the intention of the god that governed the

운 병사들의 눈에도 그무 강은 고스란히 거대한 마귀의 모습으로 비쳤다. 악마는 난생처음 맞서보는 인간과의 싸움에 노한 듯 분한 듯 발광을 하였다. 병사들이 한 발 다가서면 멈칫 물러섰다가, 다시 덤벼들기를 몇 번이고 거듭하였다.

싸움은 밤새워 계속되었다. 날씨는 완전히 개어, 다시금 찌르는 듯한 태양과 건조한 모래 바람이 휘몰아치는 사막의 아침이 밝았다. 하지만 전투는 중단되지 않았다. 밤내 싸워온 강물이 전혀 줄어들지 않았던 것이다. 병사들은 지칠 대로 지쳐 있었지만 물을 찌르고 베는 일을 멈추지 않았다. 기력이 다한 병사들은 돌을 주워다 날랐고, 화살이 떨어진 사수들은 그 돌을 던졌다. 이제 불변의 자연에 맞선 한판 싸움을 미친 짓이라고 생각하는 사람은 없었다. 그들은 다만 싸울 뿐이었다. 싸움으로 자신의 본분을 다할 뿐이었다. 상대가 강물이든 악마든 그 무엇이든 상관없었다.

삭매는 여전히 견아교착(犬牙交着)의 경계 태세가 늦추어지지 않음을 주시하다가, 마침내 결단을 내렸다. 마지막으로 힘을 몰아 마찬가지로 지쳐 있을 그무 강의

flows and waves of water. He wished to convey the fervent prayer of the people who had come a deadly, irreversible distance. However, the divine answer was not to be heard; instead, the rain poured down with more vengeance than ever. And the river got wider and more violent, its yellow muddy water reaching Sakmae, still kneeling in prayer.

"Commander! The river has swallowed up the altar! Come away, please! The longer time you take, the more furious the river god turns! Please, hurry and send the woman to the god! There is no other way than sacrificing her!"

Jang shouted, pulling Sakmae away from the river. Sakmae would not budge despite the raging water that came up to his chest. His firmly closed lips barely managed to suppress his thoughts, boiling up from the depths of his obstinate silence. His eyes were flaming with fury. It seemed that if the flame of his anger had had the power to subdue the water, he might have plucked out his eyes and proudly thrown them into the river. Overwhelmed by the weight of fear that felt so unfamiliar, Jang took a step backward in spite of himself.

Sakmae suddenly pulled his sword out of the

악마에게 일격을 가하겠다는 것이었다. 삭매는 삼백 명의 기마병을 물가로 집결시켰다. 그리고 자신의 한혈마(汗血馬)를 몰아 그 선두에 섰다. 본디 천마의 후손으로 피처럼 땀을 흘리는 푸른 총마는 주인이 갈기를 쓸어주자 비장한 각오라도 다지는 듯 콧김을 힝힝거렸다. 두려움은 부질없는 생의 집착이었다. 사랑이든 명예든 싸워 쟁취하지 않는다면 그 무엇도 없었다. 삭매는 채찍을 높이 세워들며 고함쳤다.

"전진하라! 돌격이다!"

말과 사람이 뒤섞여 절벅대며 강물 속으로 들어섰다. 강물이 주춤대며 뒷걸음치기 시작했다. 하지만 마지막 발악인 양 세찬 기세로 물밀어쳐 몇 명의 병사를 삼켜 버렸다. 삭매의 눈동자에서 새파란 불꽃이 튀었다.

"물러서지 마라! 다시 한 번 돌격이다!"

채찍을 날려 물속으로 뛰어드는 삭매를 따라 병사들은 함성을 울리며 진격했다. 그 순간, 갑자기 도망치듯 물이 빠지기 시작했다. 삭매는 승리를 알리는 뿔피리 소리와 병사들의 희열에 찬 환호성을 듣고서야 자신이 이 어리석은 전투에서 승리했음을 깨달았다. 그무 강을

sheath slung on his shoulder. Then with the sharp-edged sword held between his teeth, he glared at the sky that was completely covered with thick, dark clouds. The battle seemed to have already begun. Despite the rain beating down on his face, his furious eyes were focused on the sky as if to stab it. At last, between his lips gushed a roar that shook the sky and the earth:

"All soldiers! Into the battle formation! It is not the river god but a devil that has schemed to cause this disaster! Praying does not work against a devil. It is foolish to do so. The only way is to trust the strength of our army. With our great strength, we will conquer the devil of the river!"

Through the booming noise of the river, flowing with a vigor that could pull down even a mountain, they heard Sakmae's thundering voice. The soldiers tightened their grips on their weapons and quickly got in the fighting formation. Just then, as if frightened, the rain abruptly stopped; however, the river ran more rapidly and violently than before.

"Shoot the arrows!"

At Sakmae's command, all the archers in unison shot their bows toward the river. The arrows flew drawing an arc in the air and pierced into the pon-

희롱하던 악마는 멀리 달아나버렸다. 그러자 순식간에 홍수 물결은 사라지고 강물 바닥은 벌겋게 남은 상흔을 드러냈다.

삭매의 군대는 사라진 강물을 밟고 곧바로 진격했다. 곧이어 흉노가 치고 사는 장막인 궁려(穹廬)의 꼭두머리가 저만치 앞에 나타났다. 자연의 대재앙과 맞서 싸워 영웅적인 승리를 거둔 삭매의 부대는 말 그대로 천하무적이었다. 그들은 거침없이 흉노의 진영을 공격하여 대승리를 거두었다. 그리고 흉노로부터 빼앗은 강가의 마을에 성읍을 쌓아올려 진지를 구축했다. 삭매는 천제로부터 받은 임무를 훌륭히 수행했다. 삭매는 새로 축성한 성읍의 주인으로 입성했고, 자미는 남장을 벗고 틀어 올린 머리를 풀었다.

자미는 그곳에서도 꽃을 길렀다. 순례자의 피톨이 흐르는 그녀에게는 모든 꽃이 억겁의 인연으로 헤어졌다 만난 길 잃은 영혼인 듯하였다. 그녀는 노을에 물든 천산산맥을 천 장의 꽃잎을 가진 연꽃이라 불렀다. 황량한 사막을 연(蓮)의 꽃동산으로 일시에 바꾸어볼 줄 아는 그녀는 약간의 물과 길을 인도하는 영혼만을 따라

derous body of the river that was spewing up its yellow guts.

"Attack!"

The foot soldiers charged into the river, aiming their weapons and raising a war cry. The gongs and drums were beaten loudly to quicken their determined steps. The soldiers brandished their swords and spears frantically in the water. Both the one who gave the order and those who obeyed seemed to be possessed by something. It was a strange battle between humans and nature that could never be found in the familiar history of war. The soldiers knew that they had to win the war, or all of them would perish in the river. They shot their bows and wielded their swords and spears desperately. The battle continued until nightfall.

They stared into the dark and at the river twisting in the dark. It was no longer a river: it was a devil. Even in the eyes of Sakmae, who had been leading the battle, as well as those of the soldiers who had been fighting with all their might until they were worn out, the river appeared to be none other than a gigantic demon. The demon seemed to be frenzied and also mortified by this battle against humans for the first time. It would briefly retreat

정착하지 않는 운명을 기꺼워했다. 자미는 요염하고 화려한 여인은 아니었지만 가히 선자옥질(仙姿玉質)이라 할 만큼 기품 있고 빛나는 여인이었다. 때때로 그녀는 지상의 여인이 아닌 듯, 세속을 벗어난 아름다움으로 삭매를 매혹시켰다. 그녀와 함께 말을 달려 광활한 사막을 누비고 별 하늘 아래 잠드노라면, 능히 천하를 호령하는 영웅호걸들의 피비린내 나는 투쟁과 영토를 둘러싼 분쟁과 그 숱한 교언영색과 이전투구를 잊을 수 있었다.

꽃향기에 취해 이 년의 세월이 꿈결처럼 흘러 지났다. 마침내 삼 년째 되던 해, 삭매는 낙양에서 온 사신을 맞았다. 그동안 오랑캐의 침입이 잦아들고 교역이 활성화되어 서역에는 평화가 깃들었으니, 삭매는 속히 본국으로 귀환하라는 명령이었다. 그사이 조조는 원소의 아들인 원담과 원상의 불화를 이용하여 사주를 점령하고 중원을 통일하는 위업을 달성한 터였다. 조조는 "정치를 하는 데 있어서 덕행을 지닌 사람을 높이고, 능력과 공적 있는 사람에게 상을 주겠다"고 하명하였으니, 사신의 전갈에는 적절한 논공행상(論功行賞)으로 삭매의 공

when the soldiers took a step forward, only to pounce on them the next moment.

The battle continued through the night. The weather cleared up near dawn and once more an ordinary day of desert began with the stabbing sunlight and raging wind of dry sand. Still, the battle was not interrupted because the river they had been fighting all night showed no sign of receding. Though exhausted, the soldiers did not stop stabbing and cutting the water. The soldiers who could not fight any longer began to gather rocks and the archers who had run out of arrows threw the rocks. No one thought that the battle against immutable nature was an insane thing to do. They simply kept fighting. They were performing their duty by fighting, whether their opponent was a river, a devil, or something else.

Noticing that the soldiers were still alert in the tight engagement with the enemy, Sakmae made a decision. He wanted to channel all of their remaining strength into dealing the last blow to the devil of the Gu'mu River that he thought was as exhausted as his army. He gathered three hundred mounted soldiers by the river. On his swift-footed steed, he stood in the vanguard. His blue-gray horse, de-

을 치하하고 포상을 내리겠다는 약속도 들어 있었다.

삭매에게는 더 이상 서역에 남아 있을 명분이 없었다. 그동안 향의 하소와 여건의 청원으로 삭매의 귀환이 몇 번이고 종용된 바 있으나, 오랑캐의 동향과 불안정한 정세의 탓을 들어 번번이 체류를 연장시킨 터였다. 삭매는 자미에게 떠나야 한다는 말을 전하지 못했다. 하지만 명민한 그녀가 낙양으로부터 사신이 가져온 전갈의 내용을 알아차리지 못할 바 없었다. 자미는 번민하는 삭매의 마음을 꿰뚫은 듯 분명하게 말하였다.

"우리는 언제고, 어디든 함께 갑니다. 당신이 낙양에 간다면, 나도 그곳에 갈 것입니다. 만약 당신이 먼저 우리의 약속을 어긴다면, 당신은 당신이 몰아낸 하룡신의 복수를 받을 것이에요."

그것은 이 년 전 삭매가 하신을 무찌르고 흉노의 마을에 입성했을 때부터 빈번히 들어온 다짐이었다. 그때마다 삭매는 사나이의 이름을 걸고, 자신의 진정을 걸고 약속을 지키겠노라 맹세해 왔다. 자미는 덧붙이듯 낮고 차갑게 말을 이었다.

"당신들의 풍습이 어떠한지는 모릅니다. 하지만 우리

scended from a flying horse and known to sweat like shedding blood, neighed as if to make a grim resolve before a bitter battle, when Sakmae stroked its mane. Fear was a vain attachment to life. Whether it was love or glory they wanted, if they did not fight for and obtain it in the end, they would be left with nothing. Sakmae raised his whip high and yelled:

"Forward! Charge!"

Humans and horses ran splashing into the river together. Just then the river seemed to hold back and began to retreat. The next moment, however, as if in a last-ditch struggle, the water suddenly surged and swallowed up a few soldiers. Seeing it, Sakmae's eyes gave off blue sparks.

"Do not retreat! Charge again!"

After Sakmae whipped up his horse into the river, the soldiers followed roaring a war cry. At that moment, the water suddenly began to recede as if to run away. Only when he heard the horn sounding their victory and the soldiers' shout of joy did Sakmae realize he had won the foolish battle at last. The devil that had manipulated the Gu'mu River was gone. Then, in no time, the flood disappeared and the riverbed revealed its red scars.

는 믿어요. 강은 오랫동안 서역인들의 삶을 지배해 왔어요. 우리의 목마른 삶을 지켜줬어요. 만약 당신들이 의지해 온 미신을 따라 사람을 제물로 쓴다면, 오히려 하룡신의 노여움을 사게 될 것이에요."

자미의 경고는 저주에 가까웠다. 삭매는 문득 그녀에게 두려움을 느끼고 있는 자신을 발견했다. 꽃밭 한가운데 만개하여도 질 줄 모르고 쇠어 시드는 커다란 맨드라미, 식인귀의 입처럼, 혹은 창부의 치부처럼 검붉게 드리운 꽃술이 무서워졌다. 사랑이 식어 다하기도 전에, 델 듯 뜨거운 사랑의 공포가 악몽처럼 밀려왔다.

그녀를 두고 떠날 수는 없는 일이었다. 하지만 그녀와 함께 낙양으로 돌아간다면? 시앗을 본 향의 살기 어린 질투, 동갑의 여식 낭희를 비롯한 어린 자식들의 원망과 지탄, 한갓 저자의 입방아에 함부로 올려 찧어지는 남루한 추문에 불과해질 그들의 무산지몽(巫山之夢)이 바로 지금의 일인 양 눈앞에 훤하였다. 살아갈 수 있는 또 다른 길, 이대로 고원을 넘어 아라비아나 안식국(安息國)이나 이해(里海)로 도망치는 일. 하지만 그것은 또 다른 배신이었다. 충성을 맹세한 주군과 목숨을 걸고

Crossing the dry riverbed, Sakmae's army marched on and soon saw the tops of the tent-houses the Huns lived in. Sakmae's army, which had just won a heroic victory over the natural disaster, was unbeatable. Their attack on the Huns encampment was a great success. And in the riverside village taken from the Huns, they built a castle town as a military stronghold. Sakmae had competently and successfully carried out his duty as ordered by the emperor. He entered the newly built castle town as its lord, and Jami threw off her disguise as a man and let down her hair.

Even here, Jami grew flowers. To her, a person of pilgrim's blood, flowers seemed to be lost souls she reunited with through eons of karmic connection. She called the Tian Shan Mountains a lotus with a thousand petals. Capable of instantly visualizing the desolate desert as a lotus garden, she felt happy about her fate of an unsettled life, in which she simply allowed herself to be guided by the souls along the path blessed with a little water.

Although Jami was not a voluptuous or gorgeous woman, she possessed graceful beauty that shone through from inside. Now and then, Sakmae got smitten all over again by her beauty, which did not

그를 좇은 병사들을 스스로 저버리는 것이었다. 장수에게 죽음보다 더 두려운 것은 명예를 잃고 비천한 존재로 전락하는 일이다. 사랑을 선택한다는 미명하에 장검과 부하들을 버리고 도주한다면 싸움터에서 등을 보여 도망치는 것과 무엇이 다르랴?

아름다움은 찰나의 빛일 뿐이다. 명사산 입구를 비추는 햇빛의 요사에 사막의 색깔이 시시로 바뀌듯. 그녀가 살고 그가 죽거나, 그가 죽고 그녀가 산다면, 어떻게든 둘 다 살아남을 길이 없다면 방법은 함께 죽는 일뿐이다. 영원히, 함께하려면.

방풍림 포플러 울타리에 푸르름이 더하고, 녹지대의 밭에서 강냉이와 수수, 콩이 날로 여물어가던 초여름 무렵이었다. 멀리로부터 몰려온 희뿌연 먼짓덩이가 마침내 성문 앞에 다다라 잦아들었다. 낙양에서 온 교체부대였다. 수장은 병주 자사 양습(梁習)의 하명을 받은 장수 곽(郭)으로, 흉노의 호우들을 불러들여 관리로 삼고 흉노인을 징발하여 대군에 복속시키는 등의 파격적인 통치책을 몸소 실행하기 위해 선발대를 자청했다 하였다. 삭매는 그에게 지휘봉을 건네주었다. 이제 이곳

seem to be of the secular world, as if she herself did not belong to humanity. While the two of them were galloping through the immense desert on horseback or falling asleep under the starry heavens, Sakmae was able to forget the bloody struggles among the great heroes of the world, the disputes over territories, and the endless flattery, pretension, and base dogfights for self-interest.

Enraptured in the fragrance of flowers, Sakmae spent the next two years as if in a sweet dream. Finally, in the third year, he received an envoy from Luoyang. They brought an imperial order that he should return to Luoyang as soon as possible, since peace had settled in the west thanks to the dwindled barbarian invasions and the flourishing trade.

In the meantime, Cao Cao, taking advantage of the conflicts between Yuan Shao's son Yuan Tan and Yuan Shang, had occupied areas in all directions and successfully unified the central battle fields. Following Cao Cao's order that "under his rule, the virtuous will be honored and the competent and meritorious will be rewarded," the imperial ordinance delivered by the envoy contained the promise that Sakmae would be properly appreciat-

에는 그가 있을 자리가 없었다.

곽은 삭매보다 나이는 어리나 음흉한 자였다. 업무 인계 도중 식사를 초대받은 삭매의 집에서 자미를 보고 곽은 삭매에게 자미를 달라고 졸랐다. 분기탱천하여 단검을 빼어드는 삭매를 보고서야 곽은 자미가 주둔지의 평범한 종비(從婢)가 아니라는 사실을 깨달았다. 그는 서둘러 자신의 경거망동을 사과하였으나, 끝내 삭매의 가슴을 후비는 충고 한마디를 잊지 않았다.

"명주투암(明珠投暗)이라, 빛나는 보석이라도 갑자기 어둠 속에 출연하면 보는 이들의 눈을 놀라게 할 뿐이니! 마땅히 놓아둘 곳에 놓아두어 함께 아름다움을 즐기자는 것뿐, 노여워 마시오. 계집의 아름다움은 본디 스스로 빛날 수 없음이요, 그녀의 꽃이 과연 사막을 떠나서도 만개하리까?"

삭매는 낙양으로 원대 복귀하기 위해 성읍을 떠났다. 그 대열에는 삭매를 좇아 그무 강을 건너 흉노를 정벌했던 부대원들이 뒤를 따랐다. 물론 자미도 함께했다. 그녀는 길게 자라난 머리를 단검으로 짧게 베어 자르고 다시금 남장을 한 채 부대의 후미에서 말을 달리고 있

ed and rewarded in recognition of his distinguished services.

Sakmae had no just cause to stay in the west. In fact, he had been encouraged to return to Luoyang several times in response to his wife Xiang's appeals and Lu Gon's petitions. However, he had always extended his stay with the excuse of suspicious barbarian movements and the unstable state of affairs in the west. He could not bring himself to tell Jami that he had to leave. Nevertheless, there was no way of keeping sagacious Jami from finding out the news the envoy had brought from Luoyang. As if she had seen through Sakmae's heart, Jami told him clearly:

"We will go wherever, whenever together. If you go to Luoyang, I will come with you. If you break our promise first, you will get retaliated on by Ha'ryong the river god that you have driven away."

Jami had frequently repeated the same words to Sakmae for two years ever since their entering the village of the Huns after defeating the river god. Each time, Sakmae had sworn upon his name and integrity to keep his promise. Jami went on in a low and cold tone of voice:

"I do not know what your customs are. However,

었다.

낙양으로 가는 길목에는 다시 그무 강이 기다리고 있었다. 그 강을 건너지 않고는 어디로든 돌아갈 수 없었다. 삼 년 전 치렀던 미친 강물과의 전투는 그들의 뇌리속에 여전히 생생하였다. 하지만 보름 전 강을 건넜다는 곽의 이야기로, 그무 강이 수심이 깊고 속도가 빠른 것은 사실이나 생각만큼 대단한 강은 아니었다 하였다. 그는 짐짓 거만한 말투로 낙양까지 전해 온 그무 강의 전설적인 무용담을 폄하하려 들었다. 그쯤은 어찌 되어도 상관없는 일이었지만, 삭매는 곽의 말만 믿고 방심한 것이 사실이었다.

그들의 허세를 탓할 것인가, 운명처럼 삭매의 앞을 막아 세운 그무 강과의 질긴 악연을 탓할 것인가. 막상 삭매의 부대가 강가에 도착했을 때, 그무 강은 삼 년 전보다도 훨씬 위력적인 기세로 흐르고 있었다. 별 떨기가 뚝뚝 듣던 하늘은 어느덧 두터운 먹장구름으로 덮여, 곧 주먹만 한 빗방울을 퍼붓기 시작했다. 시시각각 강물은 불어갔다. 바람도 사납게 몰아쳤다. 하지만 삭매는 돌아설 수 없었다. 그들은 그무 강의 하룡을 물리치

we believe that rivers have governed the life of the people in the west for a long time. Rivers have kept us alive in our thirsty life. If you use humans as offerings according to the superstition you have relied on, you will only end up infuriating the river god."

Jami's word was more a curse than a warning. Sakmae suddenly found himself dreading her. The large cockscomb flowers in the middle of the garden never fell even after their full bloom; they just withered, turning tough and stringy. He became scared of the drooping dark-red flower looking like the mouth of the man-eating demon or the harlot's genitals. Even before his love for her faded, as if in a nightmare he felt overwhelmed by the horror of scalding, passionate love.

He could never leave her behind. However, what would happen if he returned to Luoyang with her? He would have to face his wife Xiang's murderous jealousy when she saw her husband's concubine, and the spite and blame from his young children, including his daughter Nang'hui, who is of the same age as Jami. He could see clearly their otherworldly love turning into a scandal to be chewed up by the people gathered in the marketplace. There was ano-

고 흉노를 격퇴하여 천하에 이름을 떨친 부대였다. 일개 병졸 한 사람까지도 모두가 역사와 자신의 삶 속의 영웅이었다. 이번에는 삭매의 의지가 아니더라도 자긍심과 명예를 건 병사들이 물러서지 않을 것이었다.

삭매는 일단 강가에 진을 치고 기다리기를 명령했다. 하지만 그날 밤부터 빗발은 더욱 거세어졌다. 복수의 다짐 같은 물살의 괴성이 밤내 웅웅거렸다. 악마는 그들을 기다리고 있었던 게다. 삼 년이라는 시간 동안 패배의 기억을 두고두고 곱씹으며 설욕전을 준비하고 있었던 게다. 삭매는 너무도 멀게만 느껴지는 삼 년 전의 일들을 아슴히 돌아보았다. 무모한 싸움이었다. 이길 수 없는 싸움이었다. 잘못하면 부하들 모두를 희생시키고 천제의 명 따윈 물거품으로 날릴 뻔했다. 이길 수 없는 싸움을 이기게 한 것은 눈먼 사랑의 마음이었다. 언제까지고 암흑 속에서만 빛날 수 있는 사랑.

그때 삭매는 젖은 침상 위에 오롯이 놓인 한 꽃송이를 보았다. 언제 꺾였는지 시들어 더욱 검붉은 그것은 맨드라미. 삭매는 갑자기 숨통이 턱 막혀오는 것을 느꼈다. 숱한 다짐, 한없는 맹세, 돌이킬 수 없는 약속. 시

ther way of survival: to elope over the plateau into another country, such as Arabia, the Kingdom of Parthia, or the Caspian Sea. However, that would be another act of betrayal. It would mean forsaking his master, to whom he had pledged his loyalty, and his soldiers who had obeyed and followed him, putting their lives in his hands. What a warrior feared more than death was losing his reputation and turning into a dishonorable man. If he eloped in the fair name of love, abandoning his sword and soldiers, how would it be different than running away from a battle, showing his back to the enemy?

Beauty is a momentary flicker of light, like the whimsical sun beating down on the entrance to Singing Sand Mountain that keeps changing the color of the desert. What if she survived him, or he survived her? What if there was no way of them both surviving? Then the only way for them to stay together forever was to die together.

In early summer, when the new green leaves were sprouting on the poplars, planted as a windbreaker around the castle town, and corn, millet, and beans were ripening in the field, a cloud of dust appeared in the distance and finally settled

든 맨드라미의 악다구니는 삭매가 자미에게 건네었던 그 모든 것들이었다. 일생의 단 한 번, 영혼을 뿌리째 뒤흔들었던 그것은 심해의 암초처럼 공명 없는 늪처럼 생의 마지막을 걸도록 부추겼다. 목숨을 건, 죽음의 도박. 애초에 누구도 이길 수 없는 싸움 앞에 그는 홀연히 맞서 있는 셈이었다.

밤을 꼬박 새운 삭매는 어스름 새벽빛을 좇아 싯누런 물결이 굽이쳐 흐르는 강가에 닿았다. 빗줄기는 여전히 삭매의 어깨를 재촉하듯 두드리고 있었다. 전날보다 더욱 불어난 강물은 승리를 장담하는 듯 오만하고 거침없었다. 이길 수 없다. 삭매는 분명한 패배를 예감했다. 그 순간 삭매의 눈에 알 수 없는 섬광이 스치며 잠시 흐려졌다 빛났다. 삭매는 즉시 막사로 돌아와 장을 불렀다. 역시 밤내 꼬박 뒤척였는지 꺼칠한 얼굴의 장이 삭매 앞에 섰다. 그는 출전 명령을 기다린 듯 단단히 무장한 차림새였다. 삭매는 한 발 장의 곁으로 다가서서, 낮지만 분명한 목소리로 말했다.

"여자를 희생시키자."

장은 자신의 귀를 의심했다. 삭매의 말을 믿을 수 없

when it arrived at the castle gate. It was an army dispatched from Luoyang to replace Sakmae's. The commander was a general named Guo, who had received an order from Liang Xi, the inspector general of Pyongju. Guo said that he had volunteered to lead the forward party to carry out some unprecedented governing measures himself, in which the powerful would be invited to serve as civil servants and some Hun men would be conscripted to serve in the large army to be stationed in the castle town later. Sakmae handed over his baton. Now, there was no position for him to stay in.

Guo was younger than Sakmae, and a wicked, treacherous man. Before the transfer of duties was completed, he was invited to dinner at Sakmae's place. When he saw Jami, he kept pestering Sakmae to surrender her to him, until he saw Sakmae draw out his dagger in fury. Then Guo realized that Jami was not one of the ordinary maidservants in the army post. He hurriedly apologized for his rash behavior, but threw in a word of advice that tore at Sakmae's heart:

"Even a glittering gem, when it unexpectedly emerges from the dark, will only startle the eyes of the beholders. I have merely suggested a gem

었다. 장은 아무 대꾸도 하지 못한 채 삭매의 얼굴을 마냥 바라보았다. 삭매의 얼굴에는 일그러진 고뇌와 회오의 빛 대신 미미한 평온의 미소마저 감돌고 있었다. 장은 침묵 속에 몇 번이고 삭매의 의지를 다시 확인하였다. 마주친 눈빛 속에서 삭매는 단호하였다. 무심히 잘못 흘린 말은 결코 아니었다.

장은 잠자코 막사를 나갔다. 그리고 묵묵히 자신이 받은 명령을 수행했다. 다시 돌아온 밤의 어둠을 틈타, 장은 입이 무거운 병사 몇을 이끌고 자미의 막사에 침입했다. 입에 재갈을 물리고 손발을 끈으로 묶어도, 아샤족 여인의 비통한 울음소리와 발작 같은 저항을 제어할 수 없었다. 삭매도 자미의 마지막 절규를 들었다. 자신의 막사 한구석에서 낙타 가죽 이불을 머리끝까지 뒤집어쓰고 두 귀를 으스러져라 틀어막고 있어도, 그 날카롭고 생생한 비명을 피해 갈 수 없었다. 여와와의 전쟁에서 패배한 분격을 참지 못해 머리를 불주산에 부딪히는 회(回)의 몸부림인 양 하늘을 찢는 번개와 천둥의 소용돌이, 천주가 부러져 기우는 듯 우지끈 쿵쾅 강물에 쓸려온 아름드리나무와 바윗돌들이 서로 부딪히는 소

should remain in its proper place so that its beauty can be enjoyed by all. So please do not be offended. The beauty of a woman cannot shine on its own. Do you think her flowers will still flourish away from the desert?"

Sakmae left the castle town to return to his home unit in Luoyang. Behind him followed his army that had helped subdue the Huns across the Gu'mu River. Jami was also among them. She had cut her long hair short with a dagger, once more disguised herself as a man, and began the journey on horseback at the rear of the army.

But on the way to Luoyang, the Gu'mu River was waiting for them again. They could not find any way of making a detour. The three-year-old memory of their battle against the deranged river was still vivid in their minds. However, according to Guo, who had crossed the same river a fortnight before, it was deep and its current swift—but it wasn't as difficult to cross as they had expected. In a deliberately arrogant manner of speech, Guo and his men disparaged the legendary account of Sakmae's heroic exploits at the Gu'mu River, which had reached Luoyang. That did not bother Sakmae; however, it was true that he had trusted Guo's

리, 성난 채찍처럼 내리치는 빗소리도 자미의 비명을 다 지우지 못했다.

날이 샐 무렵, 삭매는 부대를 강가에 집결시켰다. 병사들은 밤사이 일어난 모든 일을 아는 듯, 아무것도 모르는 듯하였다. 드러나 보이는 변화는 오직 거짓말처럼 누그러진 그무 강의 물살뿐이었다.

"진군하라!"

삭매는 도강 명령을 내렸다. 제물에 대한 화답인 양 그무 강은 어느덧 온순하게 잦아들어 발목에서 찰랑거리고 있었다. 그 물을 밟았다. 자미의 속살처럼 부드럽고 눈빛처럼 서늘한 물, 일렁임. 삭매는 아득한 현기증을 느꼈다. 비 갠 사막의 하늘은 더할 수 없이 깨끗하고 뜨거웠고, 병사들은 모두 말이 없었다. 그렇게 삭매의 군대가 그무 강을 반쯤 건넜을 무렵이었다. 앞서가던 정찰병들이 말을 멈추고 서 넋을 놓고 무언가를 쳐다보고 있었다.

"무슨 일이냐?"

"장군님! 저기를 좀 보십시오! 저것이 도대체 무엇입니까?"

word too much and so neglected preparing well for the journey.

Should he blame Guo's bluff or his long-lasting, ill-fated relationship with the Gu'mu River for blocking his way once more? By the time Sakmae's army reached the river, its force was much more formidable than it had been three years before. The stars had already disappeared, and soon, from the sky covered with thick, dark clouds, heavy raindrops began to fall. The river was swelling by the minute. The wind became violent as well. Nevertheless, Sakmae refused to turn back. His army was known throughout the world as the one that had defeated Ha'ryong of the Gu'mu River and also subdued the Huns. All members of his army, down to the rank and file, considered themselves heroes not only in history but in their own lives. Regardless of Sakmae's intention, they would never retreat now when their pride and honor were at stake.

Sakmae gave an order to pitch a camp on the riverside and wait. However, the downpour became worse that night. The menacing noise of the river, vowing revenge, rumbled on through the night. It was certain that the devil had been waiting for them all along—it had been readying itself for

그들은 강물의 상류를 가리키며 소리쳤다. 삭매도 말을 멈추고 바라보니, 과연 평원 저편에서 달려오는 무언가가 있었다. 먼눈으로 보기에 누런 용암이 흘러내리는 것도 같았고, 정체불명의 야생수가 갈기를 휘날리며 달려오는 것 같기도 했다. 그것은 느린 속도로, 그러나 꾸준하게 평원을 메우며 삭매의 부대가 도강하는 하류 쪽으로 접근해 오고 있었다. 그것의 정체를 알아차리는 데는 생각보다 많은 시간이 걸리지 않았다. 느린 꿈틀거림 같았던 그것의 이동이 금세 맹렬한 기세로 육박해 들었기 때문이었다. 곧이어 어리둥절 안절부절못해할 뿐 대처 방도를 찾지 못한 삭매의 귀에 눈 밝은 병사가 외치는 비명이 날카롭게 파고들었다.

"물이다! 홍수다!"

그제야 물이 보였다. 거침없이 밀물 쳐 침범해 드는 누런 진흙탕 물이 보였다. 홍수였다. 잠시 숨죽여 인간들을 농락했던 하신의 본격적인 반격이었다. 당랑규선(螳螂窺蟬)이라, 매미를 잡기 위해 잔뜩 노리는 사마귀는 정작 그 뒤에서 참새가 노리고 있는 것을 모르는 법인 게다. 하신은 움켜쥐었던 손아귀를 일거에 쫘악 폈다.

retaliation, chewing over the memory of its defeat for three long years. Sakmae tried to remember what had happened three years before, though it now seemed far back. It had been a reckless battle. An unwinnable battle. He might have easily sacrificed all of his soldiers and turned the emperor's command into nothing. What made the victory possible in that unwinnable battle was his blind love for Jami—love that could last only in the dark.

Just then Sakmae spotted a lone flower placed on his wet bed. It was cockscomb, withered and therefore darker red than usual. He suddenly felt choked. He had offered Jami endless reassuring pledges and promises, and there was no way of taking them back now. The withered cockscomb seemed to sling all those promises and pledges back to him. Only once in his life, his love for a woman had shaken his soul thoroughly and urged him to risk the rest of his life, as if to trap him in a reef deep in the sea or an echoless swamp. A deadly gambling! He now stood all alone facing a war in which no human was destined to win.

Having stayed up all night, Sakmae walked through the faint light of the dawning sky down to the edge of the muddy, thrashing water. The rain

골을 따라 누런 물줄기가 사방으로 흩어졌다. 어느 쪽은 빠르고, 어느 쪽은 느렸다. 하지만 여러 갈래의 발을 뻗친 물줄기는 어느 한 곳 빠져나갈 틈새를 주지 않고 삭매의 부대를 포위하고 있었다.

"후퇴하라! 일단 하류로 피하라!"

삭매는 절규했다. 하지만 이미 안전한 도주로는 어디에도 없었다. 집요한 하신의 손아귀에서 빠져나갈 방도는 찾을 수 없었다. 그럼에도 삭매의 부대는 거의 본능적으로 탈출구를 찾아 하류로 내달렸다. 낙타와 말과 사람이 뒤엉킨 채 오로지 이 구렁텅이에서 먼저 빠져나가기 위해 아우성을 쳤다. 사람과 동물이 따로 없었다. 장수와 병졸이 따로 없었다. 죽음에 쫓긴 그들은 오직 목숨 하나만이 전부인 가난하고 단순한 존재가 되어버렸다.

하지만 그 필사적인 후퇴의 행로도 머지않아 중단되었다. 모두가 거의 동시에, 그 자리에 못 박힌 듯 멈추어 섰다. 범람한 하류 쪽에서 물기둥이 솟구쳐 오르고 있었다. 이미 물에 잠긴 대지는 노여운 바다인 양 거대한 물살로 일렁이고 있었다.

was still tapping him on the shoulder as if to urge him. Overnight, the river had swollen much more than the previous day, flowing haughtily, hindered by nothing, as if to brag about its certain victory. I will not be able to beat it... Sakmae had a clear premonition of his defeat. Suddenly, an enigmatic gleam of light came to his eyes, which momentarily glazed over. He returned to his quarters and summoned Jang. Perhaps Jang also had tossed and turned all night; he stood before Sakmae with a haggard look. In full armor, he seemed to have waited for Sakmae's order to go to war. Sakmae walked up to Jang and told him in a low but clear voice:

"Let's sacrifice the woman."

Jang could not believe his ears. He could not believe Sakmae's word. Jang stood silently and kept staring at Sakmae's face. What he saw was not wringing agony or remorse, but a faint, even peaceful smile. Without a word, Jang tried to confirm Sakmae's resolution again and again. Sakmae's eyes remained focused and showed his firm determination. It wasn't that he had let slip a thought.

Jang left Sakmae's quarters in silence and prepared to carry out the order quietly. That night,

"북서쪽으로!"

삭매는 진로를 돌려 말을 달렸다. 하지만 이번에도 얼마 지나지 않아 물의 벽에 맞부딪쳤다.

"동북쪽으로!"

"남동쪽으로!"

어느 방향으로 기수를 돌려보아도 마찬가지였다. 육중한 물줄기는 사방에서 그 휘황한 장막을 펼쳐든 채 몰아치고 있었다.

"높은 곳으로 올라가라!"

물에 쫓긴 그들은 눈에 보이는 대로 가까운 곳의 고지를 향해 기어갔다. 허겁지겁 언덕을 기어오르는 병사들의 표정은 어느 전투에서보다 필사적이고 다급했다. 그들은 자신들을 급습한 홍수가 맞붙어 겨루었던 그 어느 상대보다 막강하고 냉혈하며 무자비하다는 것을 알고 있었다. 훈련된 분노, 연습된 의지가 아니었기에 더욱 그러했다. 물은 그 자체로 악하거나 화낼 줄 모르는 존재였다. 하지만 마땅히 두려워해야 할 것을 두려워하지 않는 오만한 인간을 타일러 가르치기에 주저하지 않았다. 그 주저 없음, 다만 존재로써 가르침이 혹독한 자

Jang sneaked in Jami's quarters with a few trustworthy soldiers. They gagged her and bound up her arms and legs; but it was impossible to stifle the heartrending cry of the Asha woman or subdue her fit-like struggle to escape. Sakmae also heard Jami's last scream. Crouching under the camel-hide blanket in the corner of his quarters, and covering his ears with his hands as tightly as possible, Sakmae still could not help hearing her sharp scream clearly. Even in the vortex of lightning and thunder splitting the sky—like Hoe smashing his head against Bu zhou shan Mountain on a rampage, unable to suppress his anger after his defeat in a battle with Nuwa; even in the booming noises made by the huge trees and rocks colliding with one another as they were swept down the river, as if the pillars of heaven were breaking down; even in the deafening sound of the rain pelting down like furious whips—Jami's scream was not erased.

Around dawn, Sakmae assembled his army by the river. It was not clear whether the soldiers were aware or unaware of what had happened over the night. The only change they noticed was that the river had begun relenting, unbelievably.

"March!" Sakmae ordered them to cross the river.

연의 방식이자 인간이 결코 그를 이길 수 없는 이유였다.

삭매는 언덕 위에 올라 평원을 바라보았다. 황토 강은 어느덧 드넓은 광야를 빼곡히 메우고 있었다. 시야가 닿는 곳곳이 넘실대는 진흙 바다였다. 그 까마득한 풍경이 숨이 턱까지 차올라 허덕이고 있는 병사들을 깊은 침묵으로 몰아넣었다. 아무것도 생각나지 않았고 생각할 수 없었다.

그때 아득한 서북 편 저 강 끝에, 덧없는 부표인 양 남루하게 치켜서 있는 물체가 희미하게 눈에 띄었다. 삭매는 그것이 무엇인지 확인하고자 몸을 일으켰다. 그리고 곧이어 격정 어린 탄식으로 제자리에 주저앉고 말았다. 그것은 바로 며칠 전까지 그들이 일구어 살아왔던 터전, 흉노를 내몰고 삼 년간의 꿈같은 평화를 구가했던 성읍의 성벽과 망루였다. 성읍의 모든 경지와 민가는 이미 진흙 바다 밑바닥에 가라앉아 있었다. 한낱 꿈처럼, 모든 것이 사라져버린 것이었다. 아아, 자미여, 정녕 이것이 네가 이른 저주라면.

삭매는 예감했다. 그무 강은, 진흙의 홍수는 모든 것

As if in response to the offering, the Gu'mu River had already receded a lot, now lapping around their ankles. Sakmae stepped into the water, soft as Jami's skin and cool as her eyes. Looking down at the ripples, he was swept up in an abysmal dizziness. After the rain let up, the desert was hot and the sky above was perfectly clear, and the soldiers were silent. When Sakmae's army had crossed the Gu'mu River about halfway, the scouts riding ahead of them came to a sudden halt and gazed intensely at something far away.

"Wha is the matter?"

"Commander! Look over there! What on earth is that?"

They pointed toward the upper stream of the river. Sakmae also brought his horse to a halt to take a look. Indeed, there was something rushing toward them across the plain from a distance. It looked like yellowish molten lava flowing down, or mysterious wild beasts loping toward them, their manes flying. It moved at a slow but steady pace, fanning out across the plain toward the downstream that Sakmae's army was crossing. It did not take as long as they had expected to realize what it was, because what had seemed to move in a slow

을 삼킬 것이다. 살아가고자 하는 모든 숨붙이의 욕망을 가차 없이 진흙 속에 매몰시킬 것이다. 운명의 예감, 그와 동시에 온몸이 불붙어 타오르는 듯한 분노가 그를 엄습했다. 평생을 장수로 살아온 그에게 진정한 생의 긍정은 전투, 죽음과의 눈맞춤을 피하지 않고 싸우는 길뿐이었다. 그것이 죽어도 죽지 않는 길, 지금껏 그를 살려온 힘이었다.

그는 주먹을 불끈 쥐었다. 그리고 살갗을 뚫을 듯 솟구쳐 맥박 치는 피의 힘을 느끼며 온몸으로 외쳤다.

"돌격하라!"

단말마 같은 최후의 공격 명령이었다. 삭매는 앞장서 뛰쳐나갔다. 모든 병사들이 그의 뒤를 따랐다. 그들도 이미 죽음의 운명을 온몸으로 느끼고 있었다. 비루한 은폐물에 부질없이 몸을 붙여 기대어 얼마간의 생명을 더 연장함이 아무런 의미도 없다는 것을 알고 있었다. 그들은 죽음을 향해 뛰어갔다.

"장군님! 제가 먼저 가겠습니다! 허락해 주십시오!"

장이 달려와 삭매의 어깨 너머에서 울부짖었다. 삭매는 잠시 채찍을 휘갈기던 손을 멈칫, 늦추었다. 그사이

and twisting fashion soon reached them at an alarming speed. Caught unawares, Sakmae was thrown into confusion and could not find a way to dodge the imminent danger. Then he heard a piercing cry of a keen-eyed soldier:

"Water! Flood!"

Only then did Sakmae clearly see the water, the yellow muddy water tiding toward them in full charge, impeded by nothing. It was a flood, indeed. It was the river god, who had been holding its breath to fool the humans, out to take his revenge. A mantis, too eager to catch a cicada, is oblivious to a sparrow eyeing it from behind, as the old saying goes. The river god opened his fists all at once. The yellow water branched out into many streams, filling all the gullies in the area. Some flowed fast and others slowly. Nevertheless, the flood, with its many tentacles stretched out, completely besieged Sakmae's army, allowing no room to escape.

"Retreat! To the downstream!" Sakmae cried out.

However, safe escape routes were gone. It was impossible to get away from the powerful clutches of the tenacious river god. Still, Sakmae's soldiers almost instinctively rushed downstream, looking for a way out. Camels and horses and humans all in a

를 틈타 장이 그를 따르는 한 무리의 선봉 부대를 이끌고 언덕 아래로 내달았다. 짧은 일별의 눈맞춤이 있었다. 장의 눈빛에서 사금파리처럼 빛나던 삶의 회한과 비애, 불멸의 의지, 동지애, 그리고 얼마간의 의혹과 원망과 동정.

북과 징이 울렸다. 어린 소년병은 짧은 생애의 마지막을 눈물과 함께 북소리로 울려 보내고 있었다. 함성을 울리며, 병사와 말과 낙타가 한꺼번에 탁류를 향해 뛰어갔다. 그들의 간격이 좁혀져 잠시 대치하였다고 느끼는 그 순간, 장의 부대는 어느덧 씻은 듯이 사라지고 없었다. 그 어느 전쟁터에서도 느낄 수 없었던 크나큰 공포가 그 광경을 지켜보던 삭매와 병사들을 엄습해 들었다. 하지만 삭매는 싸늘하게 얼어붙는 자신의 영혼을 끝내 용납할 수 없었다.

"돌격! 앞으로!"

달렸다. 달려 내렸다. 두려움은 곧 마지막 자존의 농간으로 적개심으로 변하였다. 끝내 지지 않겠다. 패배를 인정하지 않겠다. 하지만, 그 분노의 회오리 속에는 아련한 슬픔이 있었다. 고통 속의 평온, 무념무상 무감

frightful tangle were struggling and clamoring, bent only on climbing out of the deadly pit, ahead of the others. There was no difference between humans and animals, or generals and common soldiers. Driven by death itself, they had turned into poor and simple beings with their lives the only thing left to hang onto.

Even that route of their desperate retreat was blocked before long, however. All of them, almost simultaneously, came to a halt as if nailed to the spot. They saw a huge column of water arising from the flooded downstream. The entire area was already under water, rolling with high waves like an angry sea.

"To northwest!"

Sakmae turned his horse around and galloped. Again, however, they were soon stopped by a wall of water.

"To northeast!"

"To southeast!"

Whichever direction they took, though, they came to a deadlock. The enormous streams of water were hurtling toward them from all directions, spreading dazzling palls of water.

"Find high places!"

의 쾌락. 사막에서 삭매는 범람하는 죽음의 기운 속에 비로소 자유롭지 않았던가. 그리하여 회황색 속의 초록 신기루를 쫓듯, 일생 단 한 번 사랑에 빠지지 않았던가. 그곳을 떠나, 다시 돌아갈 곳이 있었던가.

삭매는 장검을 휘두르고 창을 치세우며 거침없이 달렸다. 조금씩 음산한 악마의 음성이, 홍수의 굉음이 귀를 찢을 듯 가까워지고 있었다. 적의 선봉은 혼탁하고도 정연했다. 전후좌우, 어디에도 결점을 찾아볼 수 없는 상산사세(常山蛇勢)의 전투 대형이었다. 포악하면서도 고고하고, 신속하면서도 서두름이 없었다. 상대를 단번에 압도하고, 스스로 굴복하게 만드는 힘이었다. 삭매는 이십여 년을 싸움으로 살아오면서도 끝내 익히지 못했던 최후의 전술을 한순간에 깨달았다. 하지만 배워 익힌 새 기술을 다른 어떤 전투에서 발휘하지 못함이 아쉽지 않았다. 이제 싸움은 마침내 끝났다.

삭매는 잠시 적의 대열 한 귀퉁이에서 자미의 모습을 본 듯하였다. 하지만 그녀는 적과 한통속으로 그를 향해 돌진해 오는 것이 아니었고, 포로도 인질도 아니었다. 그녀는 다만, 그곳에서 그를 기다리고 있었다. 끝내

Chased by the water, they ran toward a hill nearest to them. While hurrying up the hill, the soldiers looked more desperate and cornered than in any battle. They knew that the flood raining upon them was more powerful, coldblooded, and merciless than any other opponent—more so, since the river's fury and resolution were not coming from practice. Water by nature is not prone to anger or wickedness. Nonetheless, it never hesitates to remonstrate with humans about their arrogance—those who do not fear what they should fear. Nature offers harsh lessons simply by not hesitating to demonstrate its existence. It is why humans could never defeat nature.

Sakmae looked down the plain from the hilltop. The muddy river had already occupied every nook and cranny of the vast plain. Wherever he looked, there was nothing but the rolling sea of muddy water. All the soldiers, who were gasping for breath, immediately fell silent at the sight. Nothing came to their mind; they could not think of anything even if they had wanted to.

Just then, Sakmae spotted far in the distance something shabby that looked like an anchorless buoy. He raised himself to see it more clearly. Im-

배반이라 믿지 않았다고, 삭매를 향해 얼핏 웃어 보이기까지 했다. 삭매는 그녀를 향해 뛰어갔다. 그 좁고도 넉넉한 품, 비린 땀내와 향기로운 꽃 냄새가 뒤엉킨 살갗을 더듬어 달려갔다. 삭매도 그녀를 향해, 조금 일그러진 미소를 지어 보였다.

높은 탁류의 벽을 뚫고 삭매가 사라졌다. 그리고 그를 따르던 병사들과 그들의 말들과 낙타들도 사라졌다. 곧 까마득한 정적이 찾아왔다. 아무 일도 없었다는 듯, 진흙 바다는 마냥 그무 강의 아득한 하류를 향해 쉼 없이 밀려갈 뿐이었다.

* 이야기 중 '그무 강의 홍수' 전설은 중국 최고(最古)의 지리서 『수경주(水經注)』에 근거한 이노우에 야스시의 『누란(樓蘭)』(1958)에 바탕했음을 밝혀둔다.

『꿈의 부족』, 문이당, 2002

mediately, however, he sank down, uttering a bitter lamentation. It was none other than the rampart and watch tower of the castle town, the ground which they had, until only a few days before, cultivated and made a living on, where they lived for the previous three peaceful, dreamy years after driving out the Huns. All the town's fields and houses had already been immersed in the muddy sea. Like a daydream, everything had disappeared. Ah! Jami, if this really is the curse you warned me against!

An evil omen hit Sakmae: the Gu'mu River, the muddy flood, would swallow up everything, ruthlessly burying under it all living things and their desire to survive. As soon as the omen of their fate occurred to him, Sakmae felt a black rage setting his entire body on fire. To a man like him, who had lived his whole life as a warrior, the true affirmation of life lay in fighting a battle against death itself, in never averting his eyes from it. That was the way for him to live on, even after his physical death. And that was the force that had thus far had kept him alive.

He clenched his fist. Feeling the vigor in his blood that was blazing and pulsating through his body, as if to burst out through his skin, Sakmae cried:

"Charge!"

It was his last charging order, sounding like a death cry. He dashed ahead first. All the soldiers followed him. They also felt their doom instinctively. They knew it was meaningless to prolong their life vainly a bit longer by relying on an abject refuge. They charged at death.

"Commander! I will go ahead of you! Your permission, please!" Jang caught up with him and cried over Sakmae's shoulder.

Sakmae brought his whipping to a sudden halt. At the moment, Jang quickly passed him, leading a group of spearhead soldiers down the hill. Their eyes met for a fleeting moment. Sakmae saw in Jang's eyes regret, sorrow, undying resolution, comradeship, as well as doubt, resentment, and sympathy, all glinting like shards.

Drums and gongs sounded. The boy soldiers were bidding farewell to their short-lived lives in tears and the sound of drums. With a great war cry, the rest of the soldiers, horses, and camels all ran toward the muddy stream. The moment they thought they had almost caught up with Jang's group, the spearhead group, including Jang himself, disappeared once and for all. A sense of sheer horror, the intensity of which they had never experienced before in any of the battlefields, hit Sakmae and the soldiers who had just witnessed it. However, Sakmae would not allow his spirit to freeze with terror until the last moment of his life.

"Charge! Onward!"

Sakmae galloped and galloped down. His fear quickly turned into hostility, directed by his pride, or what was left of it. I will never be defeated; I will not accept it.

In the whirls of his fury, however, was a hint of melancholy. Hadn't he finally felt freedom in the middle of the desert inundated with deaths, peace within pain, and the pleasure of being unfettered from all thoughts and emotions? Hadn't he fallen in love for the first and only time in his life, as if to chase after a mirage of green in the midst of gray-yellow? If he left the desert, would he really have any other place to go back to?

Nothing could stop Sakmae from galloping toward the enemy, brandishing his sword and raising his spear high. Slowly but steadily, the voice of the devil, the deafening roar of the flood, was approaching him. The vanguard of the enemy was turbid yet orderly. Left, right, front, or rear—there was not a weak spot to be found in its tightly organized battle formation like the snake of Sang Mountain. Atrocious yet aloof, swift yet unhurried, it was a force to overpower the opponent at a single stroke into surrender of their own free will. At that very instant, Sakmae came to understand a war strategy that he had never learned throughout his twenty-some years of life in battle. However, it did not bother him that he would never be able to use the new strategy in the future battles. Now, the war was over for him at last.

Sakmae thought he might have seen Jami's fleeting image in a corner of the enemy formation. He was certain that she was not charging at him on the side of his enemy; nor was she a captive or hostage. She was waiting for him there. She even smiled at him—a faint smile as if to say she never believed she had been betrayed by him. Sakmae ran to her. He hurried into her small yet generous arms, groping for her skin that smelled of sweat mingled with the fragrance of flowers. Sakmae also gave her a slightly twisted smile.

Sakmae disappeared through the towering wall of

muddy water. Then the soldiers and their horses and camels following after Sakmae also disappeared. Soon, an endless silence fell. As if nothing had ever happened, the sea of muddy water continued to push its way toward the faraway downstream of the Gu'mu River.

* The legend of 'The Flood of the Gu'mu River' in this story is based on *Loulan* (1958) written by Inoue Yasushi, which was in turn based on *Suijingzhu*, the oldest geography book in China.

Translated by Jeon Miseli

해설

Afterword

방법적 열정

방민호 (문학평론가)

오랜 시간이 흘러도 작가의 대표작으로 남아 있으리라고 예상할 수 있을 만큼 「삭매와 자미」는 좋은 이야기의 구성 요건을 골고루 갖추고 있는 작품이다. 그러나 이 작품의 위치는 비단 작가 안에서만 가늠할 성질의 것은 아니다. 여러 지면을 통해 숱한 중단편소설이 쏟아져 나오고 있으나 썩 좋은 작품은 매우 드문 것이 오늘의 한국 문단이다. 이 가운데 「삭매와 자미」는 문체면이나 구성면, 주제면에서 근년 들어 가장 뛰어난 작품 가운데 하나로 남을 만하다.

「삭매와 자미」는 그 제목만큼이나 독특한 작품이다. 우선 이 이야기는 한국적 현실을 배경으로 한국인의 이

Methodological Passion

Bang Min-ho (literary critic)

"Sakmae and Jami" is a work so well equipped with all of the elements required for a good narrative that we can safely expect that it will remain one of the author's representative works in the future. Its significance, however, should not be viewed only in the context of the author's body of work. Although many short stories and novellas have been published in journals and other media in Korea, rarely have we lately encountered a work of the level achieved in "Sakmae and Jami" in terms of style, structure, and theme.

"Sakmae and Jami" is a work as unique as its title. First of all, it is not a story about Koreans in Korea. Sakmae is a general from Dunhuang in Gansu

야기를 쓴 것이 아니다. 삭매는 중국 후한 헌제 때 감숙성 돈황 사람으로 장수라는 것이다. 또 자미(紫薇)는 그 이름이 맨드라미꽃을 뜻하는 것으로 헌제로부터 서역 출병의 명을 받은 삭매가 끝 모를 사막 행군 중에 만난 아샤족 원주민 마을의 소녀라는 것이다. 중국에 간 한국 사람의 이야기도 아닌, 중국 땅 중국 사람의 이야기를 천연덕스럽게 풀어가는 작가.《유충렬전》이니《소대성전》이니 하는 조선 전래의 전자류(傳字類) 소설이 대개 중국을 그 시공간적 배경으로 삼고 주인공인 영웅 또한 중국 사람이었음은 다 아는 사실이다. 한국 소설이 근대화되었다는 것은 이 같은 동양적 보편주의, 중화주의에서 벗어나 명실상부 한국 적 현실에 한국인의 심성을 담게 되었음을 의미한다고 사람들은 늘상 배웠던 것이다. 그렇다면 「삭매와 자미」는 일종의 퇴행인가? 그러나 작가가 그와 같은 상식에 무지했으리라고 생각할 수 없다. 그런 점에서 「삭매와 자미」는 자신이 속한 시공간을 떠나 이야기하고자 한 특별한 의도의 소산으로 이해되어야 한다. 먼저 그 뜻을 염두에 둘 필요가 있다.

다음으로 「삭매와 자미」는 이야기 끝에 이르러서도

Province in China during the reign of Emperor Xian of the Later Han Dynasty. Jami (which means "cocks-comb") is a girl from the Asha tribe, whom Sakmae encounters during his western expedition. Thus, Kim Byeol-ah writes a story about Chinese people in China, not even Koreans in China—as if there was nothing unusual about it. We all know the Chosun-period stories, like *The Story of Yu Chung-ryeol* and *The Story of So Dae-seong*, which are set in China with Chinese protagonists. We have also learned that Korean stories containing Korean sentiments and set in Korean reality represent a modernization of Korean fiction. Then the question arises: Is "Sakmae and Jami" a kind of regression? Yet we can assume that the author was not ignorant of such common knowledge. Therefore, "Sakmae and Jami" might better be understood as a product of the author's specific intention to leave her own time and space. And it becomes our task to understand this intention.

Secondly, "Sakmae and Jami" does not clearly reveal its theme. It recounts an old Chinese story, which the author does not necessarily mean as an allegory of present-day Korean reality. The regular "hints" required in such an allegory—that the char-

그 주제를 명쾌하게 드러내지 않는 작품이다. 앞에서 말했듯 중국의 옛이야기를 했으니 그것은 오늘의 한국적 현실을 중국의 옛이야기에 빗대어 말하기 위함인가, 하면 그렇지는 않다. 그러려면 이야기에 등장하는 인물이나 사건이 그 이야기 바깥의 무엇인가를 끊임없이 지시하고 있다는 암시가 작품 내에 주어졌어야 했다. 따라서 이 이야기는 알레고리는 아니다. 그러나 한국적 현실과 암암리에 관계를 맺는 것이 아니라면 작가의 이야기는 기담에 치우친 이야기가 되리라. 한편으로 이 이야기는 제목처럼 삭매와 자미라는 두 남녀의 사랑 이야기인가, 하고 생각해 볼 수도 있다. 이야기의 대략적인 줄거리는 이렇다.

서역 출병에 나선 삭매는 자미라는 꽃다운 여인을 만나 사랑을 하게 된다. 그러나 계속된 행군 끝에 누란을 지나면서 큰비를 만나게 된 삭매의 군대는 흉노를 치기 전에 거대한 물줄기를 건너야 하는 시련에 부딪친다. 삭매의 심복인 장은 자미를 제물로 바쳐야 하리라고 간언하지만 삭매는 듣지 않는다. 그는 물줄기를 상대로 전투를 벌여 이겨내고는 파죽지세로 흉노의 진영에 쳐들어가 대승리를 거둔다. 그리고 2년의 세월이 흘러 삭

acters and events within the story represent something else in the outside reality—are lacking. Therefore, the story is not an allegory. However, if it were not related to contemporary Korean reality, as I believe it is, it might simply be an exotic story. So we wonder if this work is simply a story of a man and a woman, as its title seems to suggest.

To summarize the story, Sakmae meets and loves Jami, a beautiful girl, during his western expedition. When his troops run into a torrential rain in Loulan, they have to cross a stormy river before they can vanquish the Huns. Sakmae's adjutant general, Jang, advises Sakmae to sacrifice Jami in order to safely cross the river, but Sakmae refuses to do so. Instead, Sakmae leads his troops into a life-and-death battle with the river. After winning, his troops sweep away the Huns as well. Two years after this victory, Sakmae is ordered to return to Luoyang. Reminding Sakmae of their promise of love, Jami demands to be taken with him, threatening the river god's revenge if she is left behind. On his way to Luoyang with her, Sakmae encounter's the same, even more furious river. This time, however, Sakmae sacrifices Jami and tries to fight the river. But fate is not on his side this time, and Sakmae and all

매는 본국 귀환 명령을 받는다. 자미는 사랑의 약속을 들어 만약 그가 자기를 버린다면 물의 신의 복수를 받을 것이라고 말한다. 번민 끝에 자미를 데리고 낙양으로 돌아가던 삭매는 다시 옛날의 강을 만난다. 강은 옛날처럼, 아니 옛날보다 다 크게 울부짖고 있다. 그런데 이번에는 삭매는 심복에게 자미를 제물로 바칠 것을 명하고 거대한 물줄기를 상대로 다시 한 번 처절한 싸움을 벌인다. 이번에 운명은 그의 편을 들어주지 않는다. 삭매와 그의 군대는 홍수에 휩쓸려 사라지고 만다.

분명 작품에는 삭매와 자미의 운명적 사랑이라는 모티프가 등장하고 있다. 그러나 작품 속에서 두 사람이 맡은 역할은 그 질량면에서 매우 큰 차이가 있다는 점에서 이 이야기를 두 사람의 사랑에 관한 이야기로만 한정하는 데는 무리가 있다. 즉 이 이야기는 '삭매와 자미'라는 제목과는 달리 차라리 삭매 한 사람의 이야기라고 해도 과언은 아니다. 이야기는 삭매라는 한 변방의 사내가 전란의 와중에 공을 세워 장수가 되어, 향이라는 대부호의 딸과 결혼해 아이를 낳고 살다가, 서역 출병의 명을 받고 출정하여 흉노를 정벌해 가는 도중 자미라는 여인을 만나 사랑을 하게 되지만, 귀환 명령을

his troops disappear into the flood.

Clearly, there is the motif of a fatal love. However, this is not really a story about both characters equally, since the importance of their roles differs greatly. Despite the title, it is fundamentally the story of Sakmae: a man from a remote region who becomes a general, marries Xiang, the daughter of a wealthy family, raises children, goes on a western expedition to conquer the Huns, meets and loves Jami, eventually betrays her, and is punished on his return trip. Although Sakmae's death appears to be the price he must pay for his betrayal of Jami, it is also the fate he himself chooses. Is there an inevitability in Sakmae's need to promise his love to Jami, a lowly tribal girl? Is it inevitable that Sakmae has to sacrifice Jami on his way back to Luoyang? Although his wife and family would not welcome Jami, this was time when a general of Sakmae's stature could have many concubines without any qualms. It is only because he is Sakmae that he pours out a true love to a lowly woman and then chooses death as the price of his betrayal of this love. Who, then, is Sakmae? This question is the overriding theme of the story.

Although Sakmae could enjoy position and

받고 낙양으로 돌아오는 길에 끝내 그녀를 버리고 그 또한 홍수에 휩쓸려 죽음을 당한다는 것이다. 외견상 삭매의 죽음은 자미와의 사랑을 배반한 대가로 나타나지만, 작품의 이면을 살펴보면 그것은 삭매 자신이 선택한 막다른 운명이라고 해도 과언은 아니다. 과연 삭매가 미천한 오랑캐 소녀인 자미에게 사랑을 약속해야 할 필연성이 있었던가? 낙양에는 자미의 존재를 달갑게 여기지 않을 아내와 자식들이 있고 사람들의 성가신 눈과 소문이 기다리고 있지만 그러나 그 때문에 죽음을 무릅쓰고 지켜냈던 자미를 희생시켜 범람하는 강을 건널 피치 못할 이유는 있었던가? 상식적으로 볼 때 없다. 삭매쯤 되는 인물이라면 한 여인을 첩으로 두었다 해서 문제 될 것이 없는 시대였지 않은가. 다만 그가 삭매이기 때문에 그런 일을 벌일 수 있는 것이다. 하찮은 여인을 상대로 사랑을 쏟아 붓고 다시 그 사랑을 거둬들이는 대가로 죽음을 선택할 수 있는 것이다, 그렇다면 그 삭매는 어떤 인물인가? 이는 이 작품의 주제를 묻는 일에 통한다.

삭매는 전란 때문에 입신, 영화를 누릴 수 있게 되었으나 그 후과로 지독한 피로와 허무에 시달리는 인물이

wealth due to his distinguished military service, he suffers from an extreme sense of weariness and emptiness: "Sakmae's heart began to turn toward the nameless land far away that no one wanted and no one could own." It is at this juncture that he is ordered to go on a western expedition. While fighting against the Huns and marching through a scorching desert, Sakmae feels peaceful, though in pain: "He felt the pleasure of freedom from all worldly thoughts and emotions. If death comes to me like this, he thought, I'm willing to embrace it and stroke its dried-up bones."

Jami is a sixteen-year-old girl whom Sakmae met in this state. She is the only comfort for his heart, tired as it is of long-term solitude, which is a substitute for death. There is nobody, no outside force, except for Sakmae himself, who can take Jami away from him. When ordered to return to Luoyang, he thinks about Jami and realizes that his love for her is "love that could last only in the dark" and that "beauty is a momentary flicker of light" that would disappear under the murky Luoyang light. The life waiting for him in Luoyang exists in an artificial desert, deprived of love—a life full of murders, plunders, and political strife. He doesn't want

다. 그의 마음은 “이름도 없고 임자도 없는 땅, 아무도 소유하려 들지 않고 소유할 수도 없는 머나먼 땅으로” 치닫는다. 그리고 때마침 서역 출병의 명을 받는다. 흉노의 무리를 격퇴하고 뜨거운 사막을 강행군하면서 삭매는 고통스러우나 그 고통 속에 평온하다. 작가는 그때 삭매의 심정을 다음과 같이 표현하고 있다.

무념무상, 무감의 쾌감이었다. 만약 죽음이 이런 것이라면, 기꺼이 껴안아 그 앙상한 갈비뼈를 어루만지길 주저치 않을 것이다. (48쪽)

그리고 그때 만난 소녀가 바로 열여섯 살 자미이다. 그녀는 오랜 고독에 지친 삭매의 마음을 달래주는 유일한 위안, 죽음의 대상(代償)이다. 그런 삭매에게서 자미의 존재를 앗아갈 수 있는 외부자는 없다. 그럴 수 있는 이는 오로지 삭매 그 자신뿐이다. 낙양으로 귀환하라는 명을 받았을 때 삭매는 새삼스럽게 자미라는 여인의 존재를 되돌아보게 된다. "아름다움은 찰나의 빛일 뿐이다" “암흑 속에서만 빛날 수 있는 사랑"은 혼탁한 낙양의 빛살 앞에서 흔적도 없이 사라져버릴 것이다. 그 앞

that life, which makes him decide to drive Jami to her death and to invite on himself the river god's wrath. Sakmae fights his last battle with the river god, wagering his cold soul, which does not believe even in the power of love.

In the whirls of his fury, however, was a hint of melancholy. Hadn't he finally felt freedom in the middle of the desert inundated with deaths, peace within pain, and the pleasure of being unfettered from all thoughts and emotions? Hadn't he fallen in love for the first and only time in his life, as if to chase after a mirage of green in the midst of gray-yellow? If he left the desert, would he really have any other place to go back to?

Now, finally, we might be able to talk about the theme of "Sakmae and Jami." I believe it is a work that questions the meaning of life and suggests a way of life for readers. In the beginning, I suggested that it had a message about contemporary Korean reality. What does it mean to live as a member of Korean society, marked by the law of the jungle, political strife, corruption, and conflicts? How should we live? A life that does not pursue a noble

에 펼쳐져 있는 남은 생은 사랑이 거세된 인공 사막, 살육과 약탈과 정쟁 가득한 낙양, 그 중심의 세계에서 살아가는 일뿐이다. 그리고 그는 그 삶을 견뎌낼 생각이 없다. 마침내 삭매는 자미를 죽음으로 내몰고 물의 신에게 복수당하기를 자청한다. 사랑의 힘조차 믿지 않는 자기의 싸늘한 영혼을 내걸고 물의 신과 마지막 전투를 벌인다,

패배를 인정하지 않겠다. 하지만, 그 분노의 회오리 속에는 아련한 슬픔이 있었다. 고통 속의 평온, 무념무상 무감의 쾌락, 사막에서 삭매는 범람하는 죽음의 기운 속에 비로소 자유롭지 않았던가. 그리하여 회황색 속의 초록 신기루를 쫓듯, 일생 단 한 번 사랑에 빠지지 않았 던가. 그곳을 떠나, 다시 돌아갈 곳이 있었던가. (132쪽)

이에 이르면 「삭매와 자미」의 주제를 이야기해 볼 수 있지 않을까. 나는 「삭매와 자미」가 생의 의미를 묻고 생을 살아가는 법에 관해서 암시하는 소설이라고 생각한다. 앞에서 나는 이 작품이 한국적 현실과 모종의 관

and metaphysical value, as did Jami, the flower of a desert, would be like that of a mummy. This value could be the kind of love depicted in this story—or it could be something entirely different. This vagueness and ambiguity concerning the value gives "Sakmae and Jami" its attractiveness. By delaying the revelation of the theme until the very end, and in having the story not embody any specific theme, the author draws in readers and tells them to pursue something higher, not to believe in the mainstream order, and to live a life without fear of death. This elevates "Sakmae and Jami" to the level of a contemporary masterpiece.

계를 맺고 있고 작가가 말하고자 한 무엇이 있으리라고 했다. 약육강식과 정쟁, 부패, 투쟁으로 점철된 오늘날 한국 사회의 한 구성원으로 살아간다는 것은 무엇이며 또 그는 어떻게 살아가야 하는가. 모진 사막에 피어난 꽃 자미처럼 숭고하고 형이상학적인 가치를 추구하지 않는 삶이란 미라의 그것과 별다름이 없다. 그 가치는 이 작품이 그려낸 사랑일 수도 있고 또 다른 무엇일 수도 있다. 이 작품은 불특정한 무엇인가를 암시하는 소설인 까닭에. 그리고 이 이야기의 매력은 바로 그 불특정한 지시성, 그 애매함과 복합성에 있다. 끝까지 주제의 드러냄을 지연시켜 가면서 읽는 이들을 이야기 자체의 흥미로움 속에 이끌어 들이고 이야기의 말미에서조차 간단한 문장으로 표현할 수 있는 주제를 남기지 않는 방식으로 작가는 이 세계를 살아가는 이들에게 더 높은 것을 추구하라고, 중심이 말하는 질서를 믿지 말라고, 죽음조차 두렵지 않은 삶을 살아가라고 말하고 있다. 그 말하는 법의 독특함은 「삭매와 자미」를 근년 수작의 대열에 올려놓는다.

비평의 목소리

Critical Acclaim

최근의 역사소설에서 초점을 두고 있는 것은 어떤 인물의 '개별적 진실'이다. 이 개별적 진실은 역사소설에 등장하는 주요 인물의 복잡다단한 내면 풍경을 밀도 있게 천착하는 가운데 형상화된다. 하여 자연스레 독자가 역사소설을 통해 목도하게 되는 것은 어떤 역사적 사실의 재배치를 통한 역사의 거대심급에서 발견되는 역사적 진실이 아니라, 새롭게 인식되는 개별자로서 인간의 진실이다. 특히 우리에게 공식(혹은 비공식) 역사에서 잘 알려진 인물의 내면 풍경이 진솔하게 보여짐으로써 개별적 진실을 발견하는 일은, 역사소설을 읽는 또 다른 재미를 자아낸다. (……) 제1회 세계문학상 수상작인

Recent historical novels focus primarily on "individual truths" of specific characters. These "individual truths" are depicted through the intensive exploration of the complex inner landscapes of the main characters. Therefore, readers naturally witness not historical truths, found in the rearrangement of historical facts, but human truths of revived individuals. In particular, this author finds individual truths in the forthright description of inner landscapes of well-known official (or unofficial) historical characters. [...] *Misil*, which brought Kim Byeol-ah the first Segye Munhak Award, brings to life a Silla woman through the author's expansive histori-

『미실』은 미실이란 신라의 여성을 작가의 거침없는 역사적 상상력에 의해 되살려내고 있는 작품이다.『미실』을 읽고 있노라면, 과연, 미실이 신라의 여성인지, 아니면 현재의 여성인지 그 구분이 모호해진다. 그만큼 작가의 상상력이 미실을 과거 속에 붙들어 놓는 게 아니라 현재의 살아 있는 인물로 조명하고 있다는 반증일 터이다.

고명철, 「역사소설의 새로움을 위한 진통-김훈, 김별아, 전경린의 작품을 검토하며」, 《비평과전망》 제9호, 2005, 겨울호

이런 유형의 소설 쓰기는 매우 어려운 작업으로 판단됩니다. 그것이 왜 어려운가 하면 이미 유형화된 소설 쓰기의 한 형식으로 자리 잡고 있기 때문입니다. 그것을 우리는 흔히 역사소설로 오해하는데, 제가 볼 때는 '의사—역사소설'이나 '모델소설'로 명명하는 것이 정확해 보입니다. 이순신과 황진이의 소설화, 설화적 인물이긴 하지만 심청이나 춘향의 소설적 재해석이 최근 우리 소설계에 이미 제출된 바 있습니다. 그런데 이런 유형의 모델소설은 작품의 핵심적인 구성요소라 할 수 있는 인물, 상황, 갈등이 이미 전제되어 있어, 작가의 창조

cal imagination. Reading *Misil*, it is not clear whether the protagonist is a Silla woman or our contemporary. It is proof that the author's imagination does not limit this character to the past, but illuminates her as a human being living in the present.

Ko Myeong-cheol, "Travail for the Innovative Historical Novel: An Examination of Works by Kim Hoon, Kim Byeol-ah, and Jeon Gyeong-rin," *Bipyeong-gwa Jeonmang* [Criticism and Perspective] 9 (Winter 2005).

This type of novel is hard to write. This difficulty comes from the fact that it has already been established as a genre in the past. We often mistake it for an historical novel, but I believe it is more accurate to call it a "pseudo-historical novel" or an "illustrative novel." We have recently had novelistic representations of historical characters, like Yi Sun-sin and Hwang Jini, as well as reinterpretations of such folkloric characters as Sim Cheong and Chunhyang. In this type of the novel, the author has a very limited scope of creative reinterpretation, since critical components of the work, such as characters, setting, and conflicts, are already assumed. Even if an author's creative interpretation is successful, it takes on the nature of an adaptation

적 재해석의 여지는 그만큼 협소합니다. 설사 작가의 창조적 재해석이 성공했다고 할지라도 그것은 일차 텍스트에 대한 변용의 성격을 갖기 때문에, 비유적으로 말하면 소설적 인용과 유사한 상황에 떨어지곤 합니다.

이명원, 「서평좌담-최근의 문제작을 어떻게 볼 것인가」, 《문학수첩》, 제11호, 2005, 가을호

of a primary text. Metaphorically speaking, this re-interpretation is more or less like a quotation in the novel.

Lee Myeong-won, "Review Roundtable: How to View Recent Works Worth Noticing," *Munhak Sucheop* [Literary Notes] 11 (Fall 2005)

김별아

1969년 강원도 강릉에서 태어나 연세대학교 국어국문학과를 졸업했다. 1993년 계간《실천문학》에 중편소설「닫힌 문 밖의 바람소리」를 발표하며 작품 활동을 시작했다. 소설집『꿈의 부족』과 장편소설『내 마음의 포르노그라피』『개인적 체험』『축구전쟁』 등이 있으며, 2005년『미실』로 제1회 세계문학상을 수상한 후,『영영이별 영이별』『논개1,2』『백범』『열애』『가미가제 독고다이』『채홍』『불의 꽃』『어우동, 사랑으로 죽다』 등 역사를 소재로 한 장편소설들을 발표했다. 그 외에『톨스토이처럼 죽고 싶다』『가족 판타지』『모욕의 매뉴얼을 준비하다』『죽도록 사랑해도 괜찮아』『삶은 홀수다』『이 또한 지나가리라』『괜찮다, 우리는 꽃필 수 있다』 등의 에세이와『장화홍련전』『치마폭에 꿈을 그린 신사임당』『거짓말쟁이』『네가 아니었다면』 등 다수의 어린이책을 펴내기도 했다.

Kim Byeol-ah

Kim Byeol-ah was born in Gangreung, South Korea in 1969. After graduating from the Department of Korean Language and Literature at Yonsei University, she made her literary debut when her novella *Sound of Wind Outside of Closed Doors* was published in *Silcheon Munhak* in 1993. Her other publications at that time include a short story collection, *Dream Tribe,* and the novels *Pornography in My Heart; Individual Experience;* and *Soccer War*. After winning the first Segye Munhak Award with *Misil* in 2005, she continued to write novels dealing with historical materials, such as *Parting Forever and Ever; Nongae; Baegbeom; Passionate Love; Kamikaze Dokkodai; Chaehong; Flower of Fire;* and *Eo U-dong Dies of Love*. She is also the author of many essay collections, including *I'd Like to Die Like Tolstoy; Family Fantasy; Preparing Insult Manual; It's Okay to Love to Death; Life is an Odd Number; This Will Also Pass;* and *It's Okay–We Can Bloom,* as well as children's books, including *The Story of Janghwa and Hongryeon; Sin Saimdang Paints Her Dream on Her*

Skirt; Liar; and *If Not for You*.

번역 **전미세리** Translated by Jeon Miseli

한국외국어대학교 동시통역대학원을 졸업한 후, 캐나다 브리티시 컬럼비아 대학교 도서관학, 아시아학과 문학 석사, 동 대학 비교문학과 박사 학위를 취득하고 강사 및 아시아 도서관 사서로 근무했다. 한국국제교류재단 장학금을 지원받았고, 캐나다 연방정부 사회인문과학연구회의 연구비를 지원받았다. 오정희의 단편 「직녀」를 번역했으며 그 밖에 서평, 논문 등을 출판했다.

Jeon Miseli is graduate from the Graduate School of Simultaneous Interpretation, Hankuk University of Foreign Studies and received her M.L.S. (School of Library and Archival Science), M.A. (Dept. of Asian Studies) and Ph.D. (Programme of Comparative Literature) at the University of British Columbia, Canada. She taught as an instructor in the Dept. of Asian Studies and worked as a reference librarian at the Asian Library, UBC. She was awarded the Korea Foundation Scholarship for Graduate Students in 2000. Her publications include the translation "Weaver Woman"(*Acta Koreana*, Vol. 6, No. 2, July 2003) from the original short story "Chingnyeo"(1970) written by Oh Jung-hee.

감수 **전승희, 폴 안지올릴로**

Edited by Jeon Seung-hee and Paul Angiolillo

전승희는 서울대학교와 하버드대학교에서 영문학과 비교문학으로 박사 학위를 받았으며, 현재 하버드대학교 한국학 연구소의 연구원으로 재직하며 아시아 문예 계간지 《ASIA》 편집위원으로 활동 중이다. 현대 한국문학 및 세계문학을 다룬 논문을 다수 발표했으며, 바흐친의 『장편소설과 민중언어』, 제인 오스틴의 『오만과 편견』 등을 공역했다. 1988년 한국여성연구소의 창립과 《여성과 사회》의 창간에 참여했고, 2002년부터 보스턴 지역 피학대 여성을 위한 단체인 '트랜지션하우스' 운영에 참여해 왔다. 2006년 하버드대학교 한국학 연구소에서 '한국 현대사와 기억'을 주제로 한 워크숍을 주관했다.

Jeon Seung-hee is a member of the Editorial Board of *ASIA*, is a Fellow at the Korea Institute, Harvard University. She received a Ph.D. in English Literature from Seoul National University and a Ph.D. in Comparative Literature from Harvard University. She has presented and published numerous papers on modern Korean and world literature. She is also a co-translator of Mikhail Bakhtin's *Novel and the People's Culture* and Jane Austen's *Pride and Prejudice*. She is a founding member of the Korean Women's Studies Institute and of the biannual Women's Studies' journal *Women and Society* (1988), and she has been working at 'Transition House,' the first and oldest shelter for battered women in New England. She organized a workshop entitled "The Politics of Memory in Modern Korea" at the Korea Institute, Harvard University, in 2006. She also served as an advising committee member for the Asia-Africa Literature Festival in 2007 and for the POSCO Asian Literature Forum in 2008.

폴 안지올릴로는 예일대학교에서 영문학 학사학위를 받은 뒤 자유기고 언론인으로 《보스턴 글로브》 신문, 《비즈니스 위크》 잡지 등에서 활동 중이며, 팰콘 출판사, 매사추세츠 공과대학, 글로벌 인사이트, 알티아이 등의 기관과 기업의 편집자를 역임했다. 글을 쓰고 편집하는 외에도 조각가로서 미국 뉴잉글랜드의 다양한 화랑에서 작품 전시회를 개최하고, 보스턴 지역에서 다도를 가르치는 강사이기도 하다.

Paul Angiolillo has been an editor at M.I.T., Global Insight, R.T.I., and other institutions and enterprises, as well as a journalist and author for the *Boston Globe*, *Business Week* magazine, Falcon Press, and other publishers. He received a B.A. from Yale University in English literature. Paul is also a sculptor, with works in galleries and exhibits throughout the New England region. He also teaches tea-tasting classes in the Greater Boston Area.

바이링궐 에디션 한국 대표 소설 084
삭매와 자미

2014년 11월 14일 초판 1쇄 발행

지은이 김별아 | **옮긴이** 전미세리 | **펴낸이** 김재범
감수 전승희, 폴 안지올릴로 | **기획위원** 정은경, 전성태, 이경재
편집 정수인, 이은혜, 김형욱, 윤단비 | **관리** 박신영 | **디자인** 이춘희
펴낸곳 (주)아시아 | **출판등록** 2006년 1월 27일 제406-2006-000004호
주소 서울특별시 동작구 서달로 161-1(흑석동 100-16)
전화 02.821.5055 | **팩스** 02.821.5057 | **홈페이지** www.bookasia.org
ISBN 979-11-5662-049-5 (set) | 979-11-5662-058-7 (04810)
값은 뒤표지에 있습니다.

Bi-lingual Edition Modern Korean Literature 084
Sakmae and Jami

Written by Kim Byeol-ah | **Translated by** Jeon Miseli
Published by Asia Publishers | 161-1, Seodal-ro, Dongjak-gu, Seoul, Korea
Homepage Address www.bookasia.org | **Tel**. (822).821.5055 | **Fax**. (822).821.5057
First published in Korea by Asia Publishers 2014
ISBN 979-11-5662-049-5 (set) | 979-11-5662-058-7 (04810)

바이링궐 에디션 한국 대표 소설

한국문학의 가장 중요하고 첨예한 문제의식을 가진 작가들의 대표작을 주제별로 선정!
하버드 한국학 연구원 및 세계 각국의 한국문학 전문 번역진이 참여한 번역 시리즈!
미국 하버드대학교와 컬럼비아대학교 동아시아학과, 캐나다 브리티시컬럼비아대학교 아시아학과 등 해외 대학에서 교재로 채택!

바이링궐 에디션 한국 대표 소설 set 1

분단 Division

01 병신과 머저리-**이청준** The Wounded-**Yi Cheong-jun**
02 어둠의 혼-**김원일** Soul of Darkness-**Kim Won-il**
03 순이삼촌-**현기영** Sun-i Samch'on-**Hyun Ki-young**
04 엄마의 말뚝 1-**박완서** Mother's Stake I-**Park Wan-suh**
05 유형의 땅-**조정래** The Land of the Banished-**Jo Jung-rae**

산업화 Industrialization

06 무진기행-**김승옥** Record of a Journey to Mujin-**Kim Seung-ok**
07 삼포 가는 길-**황석영** The Road to Sampo-**Hwang Sok-yong**
08 아홉 켤레의 구두로 남은 사내-**윤흥길** The Man Who Was Left as Nine Pairs of Shoes-**Yun Heung-gil**
09 돌아온 우리의 친구-**신상웅** Our Friend's Homecoming-**Shin Sang-ung**
10 원미동 시인-**양귀자** The Poet of Wŏnmi-dong-**Yang Kwi-ja**

여성 Women

11 중국인 거리-**오정희** Chinatown-**Oh Jung-hee**
12 풍금이 있던 자리-**신경숙** The Place Where the Harmonium Was-**Shin Kyung-sook**
13 하나코는 없다-**최윤** The Last of Hanak'o-**Ch'oe Yun**
14 인간에 대한 예의-**공지영** Human Decency-**Gong Ji-young**
15 빈처-**은희경** Poor Man's Wife-**Eun Hee-kyung**

바이링궐 에디션 한국 대표 소설 set 2

자유 Liberty

16 필론의 돼지-**이문열** Pilon's Pig-**Yi Mun-yol**
17 슬로우 불릿-**이대환** Slow Bullet-**Lee Dae-hwan**
18 직선과 독가스-**임철우** Straight Lines and Poison Gas-**Lim Chul-woo**
19 깃발-**홍희담** The Flag-**Hong Hee-dam**
20 새벽 출정-**방현석** Off to Battle at Dawn-**Bang Hyeon-seok**

사랑과 연애 Love and Love Affairs

21 별을 사랑하는 마음으로-**윤후명** With the Love for the Stars-**Yun Hu-myong**
22 목련공원-**이승우** Magnolia Park-**Lee Seung-u**
23 칼에 찔린 자국-**김인숙** Stab-**Kim In-suk**
24 회복하는 인간-**한강** Convalescence-**Han Kang**
25 트렁크-**정이현** In the Trunk-**Jeong Yi-hyun**

남과 북 South and North

26 판문점-**이호철** Panmunjom-**Yi Ho-chol**
27 수난 이대-**하근찬** The Suffering of Two Generations-**Ha Geun-chan**
28 분지-**남정현** Land of Excrement-**Nam Jung-hyun**
29 봄 실상사-**정도상** Spring at Silsangsa Temple-**Jeong Do-sang**
30 은행나무 사랑-**김하기** Gingko Love-**Kim Ha-kee**

바이링궐 에디션 한국 대표 소설 set 3

서울 Seoul

31 눈사람 속의 검은 항아리-**김소진** The Dark Jar within the Snowman-**Kim So-jin**
32 오후, 가로지르다-**하성란** Traversing Afternoon-**Ha Seong-nan**
33 나는 봉천동에 산다-**조경란** I Live in Bongcheon-dong-**Jo Kyung-ran**
34 그렇습니까? 기린입니다-**박민규** Is That So? I'm A Giraffe-**Park Min-gyu**
35 성탄특선-**김애란** Christmas Specials-**Kim Ae-ran**

전통 Tradition

36 무자년의 가을 사흘-**서정인** Three Days of Autumn, 1948-**Su Jung-in**
37 유자소전-**이문구** A Brief Biography of Yuja-**Yi Mun-gu**
38 향기로운 우물 이야기-**박범신** The Fragrant Well-**Park Bum-shin**
39 월행-**송기원** A Journey under the Moonlight-**Song Ki-won**
40 협죽도 그늘 아래-**성석제** In the Shade of the Oleander-**Song Sok-ze**

아방가르드 Avant-garde

41 아겔다마-**박상륭** Akeldama-**Park Sang-ryoong**
42 내 영혼의 우물-**최인석** A Well in My Soul-**Choi In-seok**
43 당신에 대해서-**이인성** On You-**Yi In-seong**
44 회색 時-**배수아** Time In Gray-**Bae Su-ah**
45 브라운 부인-**정영문** Mrs. Brown-**Jung Young-moon**

바이링궐 에디션 한국 대표 소설 set 4

디아스포라 Diaspora

46 속옷-**김남일** Underwear-**Kim Nam-il**
47 상하이에 두고 온 사람들-**공선옥** People I Left in Shanghai-**Gong Sun-ok**
48 모두에게 복된 새해-**김연수** Happy New Year to Everyone-**Kim Yeon-su**
49 코끼리-**김재영** The Elephant-**Kim Jae-young**
50 먼지별-**이경** Dust Star-**Lee Kyung**

가족 Family

51 혜자의 눈꽃-**천승세** Hye-ja's Snow-Flowers-**Chun Seung-sei**
52 아베의 가족-**전상국** Ahbe's Family-**Jeon Sang-guk**
53 문 앞에서-**이동하** Outside the Door-**Lee Dong-ha**
54 그리고, 축제-**이혜경** And Then the Festival-**Lee Hye-kyung**
55 봄밤-**권여선** Spring Night-**Kwon Yeo-sun**

유머 Humor

56 오늘의 운세-**한창훈** Today's Fortune-**Han Chang-hoon**
57 새-**전성태** Bird-**Jeon Sung-tae**
58 밀수록 다시 가까워지는-**이기호** So Far, and Yet So Near-**Lee Ki-ho**
59 유리방패-**김중혁** The Glass Shield-**Kim Jung-hyuk**
60 전당포를 찾아서-**김종광** The Pawnshop Chase-**Kim Chong-kwang**

바이링궐 에디션 한국 대표 소설 set 5

관계 Relationship

61 도둑견습 - **김주영** Robbery Training-**Kim Joo-young**
62 사랑하라, 희망 없이 - **윤영수** Love, Hopelessly-**Yun Young-su**
63 봄날 오후, 과부 셋 - **정지아** Spring Afternoon, Three Widows-**Jeong Ji-a**
64 유턴 지점에 보물지도를 묻다 - **윤성희** Burying a Treasure Map at the U-turn-**Yoon Sung-hee**
65 쁘이거나 쯔이거나 - **백가흠** Puy, Thuy, Whatever-**Paik Ga-huim**

일상의 발견 Discovering Everyday Life

66 나는 음식이다 - **오수연** I Am Food-**Oh Soo-yeon**
67 트럭 - **강영숙** Truck-**Kang Young-sook**
68 통조림 공장 - **편혜영** The Canning Factory-**Pyun Hye-young**
69 꽃 - **부희령** Flowers-**Pu Hee-ryoung**
70 피의일요일 - **윤이형** BloodySunday-**Yun I-hyeong**

금기와 욕망 Taboo and Desire